My Next Play

An On My Own Novel

Carrie Ann Ryan

My Next Play

An On My Own Novel

By
Carrie Ann Ryan

My Next Play
An On My Own Novel
By: Carrie Ann Ryan

eBook ISBN: 978-1-950443-19-2
Paperback: 978-1-950443-20-8

Cover Art by Sweet N Spicy Designs
Photograph by Wander Aguiar

PRAISE FOR CARRIE ANN RYAN

"One of the best family romance series around! Carrie Ann Ryan brings the heat, emotions, and love in each story!" ~ NYT Bestselling Author Corinne Michaels

"Count on Carrie Ann Ryan for emotional, sexy, character driven stories that capture your heart!" – Carly Phillips, NY Times bestselling author

"Carrie Ann Ryan's romances are my newest addiction! The emotion in her books captures me from the very beginning. The hope and healing hold me close until the end. These love stories will simply sweep you away." ~ NYT Bestselling Author Deveny Perry

"Carrie Ann Ryan writes the perfect balance of sweet and heat ensuring every story feeds the soul." - Audrey Carlan, #1 New York Times Bestselling Author

"Carrie Ann Ryan never fails to draw readers in with passion, raw sensuality, and characters that pop off the page. Any book by Carrie Ann is an absolute treat." – New York Times Bestselling Author J. Kenner

"Carrie Ann Ryan knows how to pull your heart-strings and make your pulse pound! Her wonderful Redwood Pack series will draw you in and keep you reading long into the night. I can't wait to see what comes next with the new generation, the Talons. Keep them coming, Carrie Ann!" –Lara Adrian, New York Times bestselling author of CRAVE THE NIGHT

"With snarky humor, sizzling love scenes, and brilliant, imaginative worldbuilding, The Dante's Circle series reads as if Carrie Ann Ryan peeked at my personal wish list!" – NYT Bestselling Author, Larissa Ione

"Carrie Ann Ryan writes sexy shifters in a world full of passionate happily-ever-afters." – *New York Times* Bestselling Author Vivian Arend

"Carrie Ann's books are sexy with characters you can't help but love from page one. They are heat and heart blended to perfection." *New York Times* Bestselling Author Jayne Rylon

Carrie Ann Ryan's books are wickedly funny and deliciously hot, with plenty of twists to keep you guessing. They'll keep you up all night!" USA Today Bestselling Author Cari Quinn

"Once again, Carrie Ann Ryan knocks the Dante's Circle series out of the park. The queen of hot, sexy, enthralling paranormal romance, Carrie Ann is an author not to miss!" *New York Times* bestselling Author Marie Harte

MY NEXT PLAY

What happens when you fall for your best friend, but they fall in love with someone else? Nothing is what it seems in this unrequited love, new adult romance.

Miles knew Nessa never had eyes for him. Only when someone new tries to hurt her, he knows he can't stand back any longer. It's time she finds out the man he is behind the glasses and beneath the shell he wrapped himself in.

But now he has to hope that once she sees the real him, she'll stay. Because he doesn't want to let go, even if someone else tries to make that choice for them both.

One

Nessa

Music pulsated around me, and I rubbed my temples, trying to pretend that everything wasn't falling apart, and I wasn't once again falling behind. Only, that was the very epitome of who I was as a person. Someone stressed out about everything coming at them these days. Had I always been this way? I didn't know. That's what happened when the world went to hell because I thought I wanted something, only to realize it wasn't mine.

I sipped my beer and smiled down at the cup after

the first taste. It was my favorite. A blonde that Pacey had most likely picked because he was good at choosing his beer. There would be no cheap, warm brews that tasted like crap at *this* house party. At one of the other college row houses, we'd deal with whatever Keystone Light equivalents abounded. But here, there was always variety. Most of it was light beer—not enough to get somebody drunk—and not too many IPAs for people to highbrow and discuss their favorite beers while looking down on others. Pacey was good at picking his favorites, and this one happened to be mine.

Now that I thought about it, maybe that was because Pacey had been the one to introduce me to it. I needed to get over myself. And over him. Over the idea that I was in love with my best friend. I wasn't, not anymore. I'd been wrong. It'd been a crush—such an intense crush that'd crashed and burned and twisted up Pacey and Mackenzie in the process.

I'd messed up with my roommates. My best friend, my friend. And Pacey's girlfriend. I didn't need to think about the fact that the beer Pacey had chosen happened to be a favorite of mine, as well. It was a good beer. However, I needed a little more of it if my mind kept going around in this loop and had been for hours.

"I thought I'd find you over here." Mackenzie

walked over with a smile on her face. She studied mine, and I knew she was looking for any anger or resentment. But there wouldn't be. I liked Mackenzie. I respected her. And I thought she was beautiful and brilliant. And, honestly, the perfect match for Pacey—the fact that I'd had a crush on him without telling him until one of the most awkward times of my life, notwithstanding. It hadn't been her fault. And I had no hard feelings when it came to her. I just was embarrassed.

Things were awkward—at least, for me. As long as I didn't drink too much and act like a fool as I had that one night I would never talk about again, most people wouldn't notice.

Mackenzie wasn't most people.

"Sorry, just woolgathering." I took a sip of my beer. "The place is hopping tonight."

Mackenzie stood on my side in the alcove and looked around, a red Solo cup of wine in her hand. "Yes, though I didn't think the guys were expecting such a big turnout tonight. We don't have classes tomorrow, but we do have our first exams coming up, don't we?"

"Only those on a four-exam schedule," I answered, grateful we had an easy subject to talk about. "Some people only have three exams each semester or a single midterm and final. Then there are the seniors, who don't care anymore and have all perfected the skill of studying while drunk. Or are they called fourth years? What do you call college that isn't in some Ivy League and imaginary boarding school?"

Mackenzie snorted. "Have you been reading that fairy college book again?"

I blushed. "It's good. I can't help it."

"It is. That's why I told you to read it. I rarely have time to read anymore, but the audiobook was fantastic."

"I bought the hardcover. I couldn't help it. They have painted edges," I said, practically sighing.

"I saw and am a little jealous. I only have time to read while working out or driving or cooking or doing things that aren't thinking about math."

Considering that Mackenzie was a math major, that wasn't very often. Pacey's minor was in math, too. That was how the two of them had started spending so much time together—and they ended up falling in love.

I seriously loved them as a couple and still couldn't believe that I'd thought I loved Pacey the way Mackenzie did. Didn't make any sense to me. Apparently, I had latched onto the one person in my life who acted as a book boyfriend but was only the best friend.

He was a British dreamboat, but I had swooned for the wrong person.

"Did you get to the final book?" Mackenzie asked.

I looked over at her. "Not yet. I have a paper due, so I had to put down fictional fairies at college boarding schools. Which doesn't make sense because they're just training to be warriors anyway." I could go on about the book's plot and how much I loved it despite its flaws, but I held back.

Mackenzie cringed. "I have a paper coming up, as well, but it has nothing to do with math. And I kind of hate myself for letting this class wait until my final year."

"At least you didn't wait till the final *semester*. I still have a couple of gen-ed classes that I waited to fill in until this year. The thought being that I wouldn't be doing all of my difficult courses at once. Sadly, I feel like it backfired and caused me not to focus on what I want to."

"Reading can be part of your focus." Mackenzie smiled. "English majors write. And they read. I don't get to have fun in fiction these days."

I shrugged. "This semester is more about creating than reading. And it's sometimes a little daunting." I couldn't believe I had said that out loud, but I couldn't blame my words on drinking since I'd only had the one.

"If you need anything this semester, you know you only have to ask," Mackenzie said after a moment.

I nodded at her. "I know. I know all of you would. Seriously, though, thank you."

"Always. Now, I need to go find Pacey because he promised he would play a certain song, and I haven't heard it yet tonight." She winked.

I shook my head. "Go get him. I know Sasha's here tonight, so he's probably hanging out with her and reminiscing about his time across the pond."

Mackenzie rolled her eyes. "Seriously. I can't believe him sometimes. Hey, did he tell you that we might be going to London for Christmas?" She practically bounced on her toes.

I blinked. "Really?" I asked, trying not to let my voice squeak—I think I failed.

Mackenzie was too excited to notice. "Yes, his dad and his girlfriend—or Pacey's new stepmom, I guess—went back to London, and I know Pacey is trying to work things out. By Christmastime, there'll be a new baby. Pacey was thinking of heading over there for the holidays and asked me to go with him."

"That's a huge deal, and that's awesome," I said, meaning it.

"I know. Somehow, his father invited my parents. Now, it's a whole thing," Mackenzie said with a wince.

That *was* a whole thing, but it sounded nice. Like a real family. "Interesting." I held back a laugh at the look on my friend's face.

"We're trying to make it work. I don't know. But I get to see London. And Big Ben and all of that. I'm just excited. As long as I get to spend the holidays with Pacey, I'm happy."

"It'll be fantastic. Just pack me away in your luggage where you can." I nearly winced at the awkwardness.

"You know, I'm sure…" Mackenzie began.

I shook my head. "No. There's no way I can afford it, nor will I let anyone pay for me," I countered quickly before she could add anything. "And don't worry. I'm probably going to have tons of other things to work on. Plus, the bookstore still has holiday hours during that time."

"Okay, sorry, I didn't mean anything by it," she said. "I'm such a dork."

I shook my head. "It's fine. I'm fine. Now, go find Pacey. Get that song. I am going to get another beer. And then maybe I'll head home and work on that paper."

She raised her brow. "Working while drinking? That's not normally like you."

"I'd say I'm turning over a new leaf, but that would probably be an issue if it were true. I need to think about what I want to write. Since it's not coming to me, I'm going to enjoy myself. It's not as if the paper is due tomorrow."

She studied my face and then nodded. "Okay, I guess I'm going to go."

"Go," I said, hating the tension. It wasn't Mackenzie's fault. It was mine. My friend smiled softly before heading to Pacey, and I let out a breath, telling myself to cut out the bullshit and be happy.

I looked down at my empty cup and figured I needed another beer. Or four. I could probably sleep on someone's couch. Or, one of my other roommates —Natalie or Elise—could get me home. Of course, Elise and Mackenzie were probably spending the night here since they were dating people who lived in the house. I'd have to find Natalie and make sure she got me home safely if I drank too much. Or I could Uber it, I guessed. It didn't matter. I could take care of myself. I always had, and I always would.

I turned the corner and ran into a very hard chest, looking up to see Miles. He had his glasses on, making his face look far hotter than I'd let myself notice before, and I blinked up at him.

"You're wearing your glasses," I blurted. I could have rightly kicked myself.

His lips quirked into a smile, and I did my best not to look at them directly. I remembered the last time I had been up close and personal with Miles' mouth. Only no one knew I'd been so close to those particular lips. And no one ever would. I did my best to pretend I didn't remember, and he hadn't mentioned it. I had been drunk—oh, so fucking drunk—and had made one stupid decision after another.

I'd felt poorly about myself; like I couldn't do anything right. It hadn't helped that my life had changed instantly, and it had nothing to do with school and everything to do with what I had been hiding from even myself.

I'd had too many drinks that night. Had nearly gotten into a very compromising situation with a guy whose name I still didn't remember and ended up practically falling on the floor in front of Miles. He had tucked me into bed and kept me safe. And when I had wanted to change everything, to prove that I was fine—even though I hadn't been anywhere close—I had kissed him. Right on the mouth. Sweet and hot and so wrong. A horrible mistake that I wouldn't make again.

Miles was *nice*. He was a nice guy without being the token *nice guy* who believed he needed and deserved every girl he was nice *to*. He was just a good guy. And maybe that was a better descriptor for him. He was a good guy. A good person and a good man.

I would pretend I had never kissed him because it was already awkward as hell. Why shouldn't I continue being uncomfortable?

"It was a high pollen day, and I didn't feel like

putting in my contacts. I do wear glasses. You've seen them," he said, his voice low.

The other roommates, Dillon and Tanner, always said that Miles was the nerdy one, mostly because Miles *was* their nerdy roommate and had given himself the label. His glasses and maybe his hobbies were the only nerdy things about him, though. He was tall, built, broad with muscle, and hard…everywhere.

That thought just made me blush harder, and I did my best not to think about exactly what was hard and where it was on him. I would not think about that. That would send me down a path to destruction and make me feel as if I were losing my damn mind. I had already fallen down the rabbit hole of falling for someone I shouldn't.

I did not need to make it a problem again, where I fell for someone who just so happened to be nice to me.

I wasn't *that* pathetic.

Yet, those glasses? They did things. Warm things.

Perhaps one beer was enough, after all.

"Oh, I like them. Anyway, thanks for catching me since I probably would've tripped over my feet turning the corner so quickly."

He swallowed hard, and I did *not* look at how his neck moved. I did not. "I ran into you, too. I'm sorry."

"Don't be. It's your house."

"It is my house. That means I get to just run into everybody?" His cute brows furrowed.

Cute? How could brows be attractive? Was I placing my crush from Pacey onto Miles? That was the only explanation. And…I was an idiot. A pathetic loser idiot who needed to go home and write her paper and pretend that I had my life under control.

That would make much more sense.

"I guess I'm going to head home." I hadn't meant to say that aloud.

"Did I hurt you?" He pushed up his glasses as he studied my face.

Why was I watching his forearms as he pushed up his glasses? What was in that beer?

"No, I just have a lot on my mind. And homework. And I should probably stop at one beer." Not a lie.

"I thought you were on your way to the kitchen to get more. You don't need to leave because I ran into you."

"It's not about you. I promise."

His cheeks blushed, and I wanted to kick myself. Why was I such an idiot? Every word that came out of my mouth felt as if I was kicking him. I didn't know why. "I didn't think that. I should go."

I reached out and gripped his forearm. His *thick* forearm. All muscle. The muscle I wasn't going to think about. "Sorry, I'm having an off night."

Or an off *life* at this point.

"I can see that. I'm having one, too. I *am* sorry that I ran into you."

"You don't have to be sorry, and not just because you live here. We were going around blind corners. I'm surprised it doesn't happen more often. Anyway, it was nice to see you, Miles," I said, very proud of how I sounded—like an adult without issues plaguing them.

He let out a breath. "Have a good night."

"You, too, Miles," I said, feeling his gaze.

I couldn't let on that I knew. That I remembered kissing him.

I didn't know if he'd kissed me back. Though perhaps I didn't want to know. I needed to stop thinking about dating within the house pool. I needed someone new. Somebody who made me smile and laugh and didn't live at the same address as Pacey, Dillon, Miles, or Tanner.

There were many guys at school. They existed; I knew they did. I didn't need to think about Pacey. Or now Miles, it seemed.

Miles looked at me again. "Sure." Then he headed over to a group of people I knew shared his major. Since we were all starting our senior years, most of us ended up in groups of people we studied with.

English majors were a little different because there were enough of us, like the business majors, who ended up in our own little worlds, usually alone. I had my roommates. I didn't need anyone else.

I ignored my earlier thought about another beer and once again considered going home, but then I would just be running, wouldn't I? Also, I didn't want to be a liar.

My phone buzzed, and I pulled it out of my cross-body bag and frowned.

Dad: *Just checking in on you.*

My eyes burned, but I didn't cry. I didn't do anything. I didn't have a lot of feelings left. Or maybe the problem was that I had too many.

Me: *Everything's good. I love you, Dad.*

Dad: *I love you too. Just miss you.*

Tears nearly fell again. I blinked them back. I did not need to think about my home life. I didn't need to think about anything beyond school.

It was just Dad and me now. Cancer had finally taken Mom after a hard and painful fight. It was only the two of us left. *He* was the man I needed in my life—no one else.

He was alone tonight, and so was I—even surrounded by people.

Me: *I love you. I'll call you tomorrow?*

Dad: *I'd like that. Stay safe, buttercup.*

I snorted at the nickname and then smiled.

Me: *Always.*

I put my phone back into my purse, grateful I hadn't cried in the middle of the party. Tanner was off in a corner, his harem of people around him. I didn't know if he was in a relationship or not since the triad he had been in had blown up because of cheating—though not by Tanner. He had rules. And if you broke them, you were out of his life.

He met my gaze over the throng of people and raised a brow. I shrugged, threw a little wave, and headed towards the door. Natalie and Elise were off in another corner with Dillon and a couple of people I didn't recognize, but they didn't notice me walk by. They were all having an animated conversation. I kept moving, not wanting to intrude, especially with the dark cloud above my head.

I didn't know where Pacey or Mackenzie had gone, and I did my best not to look for them. I would text everyone that I was headed home so they wouldn't worry.

Even if I felt alone in a crowd of people, my roommates and the guys would always make sure I was safe. I had them in my corner, and I had to remember that.

Closer to the door, I ran into another person. My shoulder ached, and I winced. Tonight was so not my night.

I looked up at the man with blue eyes, blond hair

that curled over his shoulder, and a smile that had two dimples peeking out of his cheeks.

Okay, then. *Swoon.*

A nice guy. One smiling at me and giving me a very come-hither look. And he did not live at this address.

"I'm sorry," he said, smiling down at me. "I didn't mean to bump into you."

I smiled back. "I'm sorry, too. I seem to be clumsy today."

"You, clumsy? Oh, I don't think so. Maybe it was just meant to be that I knocked into you." He winced. "Wow, that was possibly the worst line I've ever used. I could have said something about, 'Did it hurt when you fell?' but that would be going too far."

I laughed, shaking my head. "I'm glad you didn't start with that."

"Are you heading out?" he asked. "I hope not."

"Another line? A little smoother this time, at least. As for leaving, I'm not sure yet."

"I'm Xander. You should come and have a drink with me. To say sorry for knocking into you."

"I'm Nessa. You know what? Maybe a drink is okay."

"I like the sound of that, Nessa." Xander held out his arm. I linked mine with his and laughed.

Tonight had not gone exactly as I'd wanted it to,

but Xander seemed nice. At least for a beer and a laugh.

He didn't live with Pacey, he *wasn't* Pacey, and he wasn't a guy with glasses that I seemed to have imprinted myself on, one I had kissed when I was at my lowest. A guy who'd been so sweet to me, I was afraid that I would hurt him unintentionally by being myself.

I pushed thoughts of Miles out of my mind and had a beer with Xander.

This year was supposed to be about being a new Nessa. About new beginnings and trying to pull myself from the ashes of before.

Somehow, I'd find a way to make that happen.

Even if I wasn't sure if the embers had thoroughly doused themselves along the way.

Two

Miles

"You're telling me you're almost done with college, and you still don't have a girlfriend?"

I barely resisted the urge to roll my eyes at my younger brother as he bit into a French fry and grinned at me.

Aaron was fourteen. He'd been the surprise baby my parents hadn't expected. After all, they had already been raising twins and hadn't been prepared for a third kid. But along came Aaron, and our family was complete.

At least, for as long as we'd had it.

Aaron was loud, mischievous in the best ways, loved video games, and was a history nerd. However, he did his best to hide that from the rest of the world so he didn't get bullied in school. He had plans to use history and some form of media to take over the world. I wasn't a hundred percent sure how that would happen, but the kid wanted to go to college when the time came, and I was sure he would find a major that worked. It had taken me a while to figure out what I wanted to do, and here I was, in my senior year of college, getting a biomaterials degree, with grad school in the future and all of the lovely paperwork for my course load. And no girlfriend.

A fact that Aaron liked to point out.

Often.

"Hey, you don't have a boyfriend," I said. Oh, good. Now, I was kicking at a teenager to make myself feel better. Just kill me now.

Aaron only grinned. "That you know of."

This time, I did roll my eyes. "If you did, you'd have told me."

"That's true," he said, dipping his French fry into his milkshake. I did the same and sat back in the booth. We were sitting in a diner near campus, spending what little time I had in the afternoon just hanging out. I rarely got time alone with my brother without my parents breathing down my neck, being their overprotective selves. Not that I blamed them given everything that had happened, but it wasn't like I could do anything beyond seeing Aaron for a couple of hours a week—if that.

I had made my choices before, and I had to live with them. I hated that Aaron had to live with them, as well.

"Seriously, why don't you have a girlfriend? Weren't you dating that one girl from your class?"

I bit into my burger, giving myself time to answer. "We're just friends. Well, I thought we were friends. She wanted to get some things off her checklist," I said, thinking of Marie. She'd wanted to spend a few weeks together for her plans, though I'd only featured in them marginally. She also fought the curve with me in every one of our upper-level classes.

"You mean she wanted to lose her V-card before she finished school?" My brother whispered the words, but they seemed to echo throughout the diner.

I cringed. "There were so many things wrong with that statement. However, the two of us weren't on the same path into what we wanted out of a relationship."

"You want love and marriage and all that?" Aaron asked.

I wanted to reach across the booth and smack him

on the back of the head. I refrained. Only barely. "Not exactly. But it's fine. We're still friends."

"Isn't she in all your classes, though? You said you only had like eight people in each of your senior-level classes. That's what you said."

The kid never forgot a thing I told him. "Yes. And she's dating one of the girls in our class now. They're happy. I think they're going off to grad school together."

"So, you got left behind. Poor guy. It's okay. I can teach you my moves."

I snorted. "You're fourteen. I don't want to know what your moves are."

Affronted, Aaron puffed out his chest. "I've got moves."

"You'd better not, or Mom and Dad will bring down the hammer," I warned, not teasing this time.

Aaron winced. "Okay, I don't have moves. I have friends. No moves. You know Mom and Dad rarely let me out. I swear, if you hadn't arranged this whole lunch thing on the weekends for us, I don't think I'd even get to see you."

I held back a sigh. "I'm always here, Aaron. No matter what. You know Mom and Dad are only over-protective and strict in their rules because they love us."

"Yes, because of…well…everything."

I swallowed hard and reached out and gripped his wrist. "I'm sorry, you know? That you have to deal with my messes."

Aaron's throat worked as he swallowed hard, but he looked up at me. "Don't be sorry. I don't blame you, you know. For anything."

Tears pricked the backs of my eyes, and I let Aaron's wrist go before I leaned back in the booth. The half-eaten burger in my stomach felt like lead, and I wasn't hungry anymore. I pushed my plate to the middle and ignored my melting shake. "We all make decisions, and we all face the consequences." *At least those who survive the decisions*, I thought to myself, but I didn't say that out loud. Only I knew Aaron thought it, too. After all, it had only been four years ago when everything had changed. Aaron was fourteen now, in his first year of high school, and things were changing even more.

Our parents were strict with him, far more stringent than they had ever been with us. They tried to impose the same rules on me now, even though I wasn't a child anymore. All because of one night when I hadn't said no. When I had given in.

I sighed and pushed the thoughts from my mind. I didn't need to think about that. As it was, I had applications to work on and essays to fill out. Grad school wouldn't pop into existence on its own. I needed to work on programs that would pay me a stipend and allow me to go to school. I had earned scholarships for undergrad. Had saved throughout high school and college, and my parents saved for me so I wouldn't end up in debt when it came to school. I was a teacher's assistant on the side, which helped with bills, but I was still lucky. The grants I had now meant I needed to prove that I was worth it later. Special compensations wouldn't pop out of nowhere.

"Hey, is there a reason we came here instead of meeting at your place?" Aaron asked after a moment.

I pulled myself out of my thoughts. "Oh, Tanner was in a mood, and I didn't want to deal with it."

"At least, he's better than the guy you were sharing a room with when you were in your dorm your freshman year."

Freshman year had been a mistake. I had received full room and board that first semester and had told myself I was ready to deal with real life. That I didn't need to live with my parents. That even though everything had just happened and was so fresh, the wounds still bleeding inside my heart, it was only metaphorically.

My roommate had ended up stealing from me, acted like a douche, and constantly locked me out. He hadn't liked that I enjoyed reading, science, or things having to do with life outside of *banging chicks*—

at least, according to him. Everything that I had done, even wearing glasses and liking superhero movies, had been too geeky for him, and he'd made sure I understood that. Superhero movies weren't only for geeks anymore. They were popular culture that everybody liked. Yet, I had been a nerd to him, so he thought I deserved to get my shit stolen and broken.

Between dealing with my roommate and everything at home, my parents had pulled me out of the dorm, and I ended up living with them for a couple of semesters until I couldn't take it anymore. Then, I'd been lucky enough to find a place with Dillon, Pacey, and Tanner, as well as Sanders.

Sanders no longer lived with us and was a complete asshole. I was grateful he was gone. He had always had a stick up his ass and had treated me much like my old roommate had. When he ended up cheating on his girlfriend, Mackenzie—who now dated Pacey—Sanders had ended up leaving to live in an apartment that his parents paid for. My parents helped pay for school so I wouldn't begrudge him that. However, the fact that he lorded it over us even after he cheated on a girl we all liked? *That* pissed me off.

"Tanner's being a jerk, so I can't come over..." Aaron said, wiping his hands after he'd finished his meal, still eyeing my burger. I sighed and shoved the basket at him, and Aaron began devouring it. He was a growing boy. I didn't blame him.

"He's dealing with some shit, so I'm just going to let him wallow in his feelings for a bit. He's not a jerk. He's having a tough semester, and I figured he could use some space and time alone. The other guys are out today."

"With their girls?" Aaron asked, and I rolled my eyes.

"Pacey is. I think he's at the girls' house now, working on something. Dillon, however, is at the family's bar."

"I want to go there and see it," Aaron said.

I laughed outright. "Yes, because I can just imagine Mom and Dad letting me take you to a bar."

"They serve food there, don't they?"

"Yes, they do. Some of the most amazing food I've ever had. But I'm still not taking you."

"You're no fun."

Even though I knew he was teasing, I made sure Aaron met my gaze as I spoke. "I'm not taking you to a bar. You know why."

I hated having to do it, making him remember. But there were reasons our parents were overprotective, and I had to make sure he thought about those things and didn't set them off.

My parents weren't cruel. They didn't yell. But they

were broken inside and always would be until they learned to heal. Though I didn't think they wanted to. Somehow, I had pieced myself back together, even though the jagged remains still cut every once in a while. My parents may never find a way to sew themselves back together.

"I'm sorry. I didn't think." Aaron's voice was so small I wanted to reach out and tell him that everything would be okay, even if I didn't believe it.

"I hate that you even have to. I don't want you to ask Mom and Dad out of the blue because you want to see Dillon's place. You'll end up hurting them in the end. You know?"

"I do. I'm sorry."

"Don't be. Seriously. Speaking of, Mom and Dad will be here to pick you up any minute."

"I guess I should go wash my hands so I'm not covered in grease."

"Yes, let's do that."

Aaron got up, stuffed the rest of my burger into his mouth, and went to the restroom to wash his hands. I cleaned up the table a bit and made sure I left a big tip for the waitress.

I had waited tables my first two years of college because I needed money for school and other things. Somehow, I'd made my way through, even broken, but over the past year and a half or so, I had been lucky in that I had gotten a job at the school. I was a TA and made the same money I had when I'd waited tables at a diner much like this one. I knew Pacey worked off and on, though he had taken the last semester off because he had gotten sick. Dillon worked hard at his family's bar, and I knew Tanner worked, too, though he didn't talk about it. If I remembered correctly, he'd said he was a bouncer somewhere, but he also worked odd jobs at strange hours because he was saving up as much money as possible.

Either way, all of us did our best to focus on what we could to make money for our futures and to figure out exactly who we wanted to be when we left the hallowed halls of college.

Aaron returned, and I nodded at the waitress as we headed out to the parking lot. My parents were waiting, slight smiles on their faces.

"There you are. We were thinking of heading to one of the antique shops on the way home. What do you think, Aaron?" Mom asked as she kissed the top of his head, though she barely had to bend down to do it. Aaron wasn't a baby anymore and was nearly as tall as I was.

My mom ran her hands through his hair, and he grumbled but let her do it anyway. I moved closer to her and wrapped her in a hug. My parents might want to control my life sometimes and make things difficult and awkward, but I loved them.

She hugged me tightly and kissed my cheek. “Look at you. I swear you’re getting more muscular. Like a real man.”

Aaron snickered.

My father sighed. “Please, think about what you say before you speak, darling,” he muttered under his breath as he squeezed my shoulder. “But you *are* looking good.”

“Thanks,” I said, blushing hard.

“Why are you wearing your glasses? Did we not set you up for your new prescription for your contacts? Here, let me look in my phone. I can make you an appointment with Dr. Morgan.”

“No, I’m fine. I’ve just had some bad allergies recently and have been wearing my glasses more. It’s good for my eyes to let them breathe.”

“Allergies?” mom asked as she frowned. “Have we looked into the allergist recently?”

“We have. I promise. Thank you, Mom. I have all my appointments set up on my phone.”

“They’re not in mine. You should sync your calendar with mine like I keep saying.”

Then my mother would know where I was at all times. She would be happy with that, but I was an adult. I loved her and knew there were reasons she was this overprotective, yet I needed to set boundaries.

Even if it pained me to do it because of the look in her eyes.

"I need to head out. I have papers to finish, homework to work on, as well as some applications to complete."

"Are we still talking about the same eight colleges?" Dad asked, and I nodded.

"Yes, they have the best programs for me and high financial aid and stipends. That's the goal."

"You're going to do great, wherever you go. Although, if it could be CU, that would be wonderful," Mom said, giving me a pointed look.

Anywhere that was in the state and not too far away, where they could drive down the road to me? Yes, that would be perfect for them.

It didn't matter that I explained that going to schools in different states in entirely different programs looked best for jobs if I wanted to go into academia—though I wasn't sure I did. I had already mentioned it more than once, but nothing I said would change her mind. There *was* a perfect in-state school, but it was hard to get into.

As it was, I looked over at Aaron, and he just gave me a small wave. Even though I knew me branching out on my own and going to grad school in a different state would be good for me, I would be leaving my little brother, and that wasn't something I was sure I could do.

"Drive safe. Text me when you get home."

"Mom..." I began.

Dad frowned. "Just do it. It'll help all of our nerves."

I sighed and nodded. "I can do that."

I hugged my parents, messed with Aaron's hair just because I could, and then watched them drive away. I loved my family. There was no stopping that. And they might want different things than I did, but they had always been there for me, even when my mistake had changed everything. Only, as Aaron had said, maybe I needed a life. Or at least a girlfriend.

As if I had conjured her from thin air, I heard her laugh.

I looked up as Nessa walked across the parking lot, a guy who looked somewhat familiar by her side. They weren't holding hands or even touching, but they were walking close enough that I knew it was probably a date. An afternoon outing at the same diner I had just eaten at. Nessa didn't notice me—she never did.

I was always only the roommate, the friend. The guy she had kissed one night and didn't remember. I wasn't going to be the one to remind her. She wouldn't have done it if she had been in her right mind, and I hadn't kissed her back. I wouldn't have. She had been drunk, and it would have been stupid.

That didn't mean I had forgotten it. At all.

Now, Nessa was out with someone, clearly over Pacey. Even in her busy schedule, she'd found time to have a life. My little brother was right. I *did* need a life. And I needed a girlfriend.

Someone who wasn't Nessa.

THREE

Nessa

Books made everything better. At least, that's what I told myself after the week I'd had. I looked over my shoulder to make sure nobody was watching before I gently sniffed the book in my hand, inhaling that new-book smell. Everything felt better when I had a book in my hands and near my soul.

"Are you smelling the books again?" Everly asked as she walked over to me, a broad smile on her face. She'd tied her hair back and had on a cute, flowy top over leggings. She was gorgeous. One day, I wanted to be her.

"Maybe…" I blinked innocently, and the other woman just grinned.

"We at Beneath the Cover believe that sniffing your books is the best way to start your day."

"I'm glad I'm working at the right place." I winked, and Everly laughed.

Beneath the Cover was a small bookshop in downtown Denver that the owners had rebuilt after a fire years ago. It had been my favorite place to come when I was in high school, somewhere my mother and I visited often before she got sick. When they rebuilt it, and quickly thanks to Everly's husband's family business, the place had thrived.

When I wasn't at school or studying, I was here, at this bookshop or across the street at the café I liked to visit. That was also part of Everly's family's business somehow. I also visited a little boutique and even a tattoo shop where I had gotten my first and only tattoo—a little bumblebee on my wrist.

My dad had rolled his eyes and shook his head when he saw it. The ink had been for Mom, so he had gotten a bumblebee, as well, on his forearm that blended with his other ink. Montgomery Ink had taken care of us, and now, I was working at their family's bookshop.

I knew that Dillon's family was somehow connected to them, too, though every time I tried to think about it, my eyes crossed. But I knew that the Montgomerys were everywhere. However, what mattered to me right now was this bookshop and that Everly was always here for me.

"I'm almost done stocking the fantasy section."

"Good, you're doing a great job of it. I love the display you did up front."

"I do, too. The color cascade worked out well."

"It's like in a library when people say, 'I don't remember the title, but the cover was blue.'" Everly rolled her eyes. "We have an ombre blue section now. Perfect for our needs."

"I saw it on a meme." I shook my head. "I didn't make it up."

"I'm pretty sure I saw the same one but in yellow. We do what we can. Business is going well." Everly winced and knocked on a wooden bookshelf. "That means I need to go in the back and get some work done."

"No problem. I'll work up front."

"You're not alone, but I'm delighted that you're here." She reached out and squeezed my shoulder before walking back to her office. Everly had been through hell, though I didn't know much about it, just rumors and things she had let slip. She was so strong. Marriage, family, and having her own business had done well for her. She knew where she was and who she needed to be. In contrast, I felt as if I had no idea what my plan should be.

My phone buzzed, and I looked around. Everly didn't care if I responded to a text as long as there weren't customers waiting for me and I got my work done, but I still made sure no one was watching.

Xander: *Just making sure you're having a good day. Will I see you tomorrow for our date?*

I bit my lip and tried to feel that warm feeling, the little buzz in the gut that told me this was the guy for me. Only, I wasn't sure. Xander and I had gone to the diner for our date, and it had been nice. He was pleasant, the food was decent, and he'd made me laugh. There was just no zing.

My problem was that I had felt a zing twice now with two people I shouldn't. That meant I probably shouldn't trust my zing.

Still, I would go on another date and wonder what zing I should be looking for and ignore the ones I'd already felt for the wrong people.

Me: *I'll be there.*

Xander: *I had a good day. I hope you did too.*

Me: *Totally. Only now I'm working. Talk to you later?*

Xander: *No problem. Call when you get home?*

I frowned but shrugged.

Me: *Maybe. Got to go.*

After one date, I wasn't sure I was comfortable telling him where I was at all times, but I understood that he wanted to make sure I was safe. It would be after dark in downtown Denver for the drive south to the campus area where I lived. Our campus wasn't downtown like a few of the major ones were, but it was close enough. Just a quick jaunt down the highway. And, thankfully, it would be after rush hour. Although, I sometimes felt like rush hour in Denver was every hour.

I slipped my phone back into my pocket and returned to work. I helped a few people check out, found books they wanted, and then went to my other display in the kids' section.

There was more staff on hand. Miley worked up front and was hyper and bubbly at the register. People were usually drawn to her, which meant I could do more stocking, arranging shelves, and making recommendations. I liked that part better, anyway. In the end, my to-be-read pile went insane. As if it'd multiplied when I wasn't looking.

The bell above the door rang, pulling my attention from a stack of books about a fox that liked to play with a deer. I looked over my shoulder and smiled as Mackenzie, Elise, and Natalie walked in. My roommates gave me a quick wave, said hello to Miley, and then headed my way.

"Hey, there." Natalie smiled at me and hugged me as Mackenzie and Elise moved around to do the same.

"I didn't know you guys were coming in today."

Mackenzie shrugged, a smile on her face. "I had that seminar at UCD, so I was already here. And Elise was visiting with Dillon at the family's brewery. It just made sense for us to come."

"And I tagged along," Natalie said with a laugh. "However, I got to have magnificent wings at the brewery."

My stomach growled, and I put my hand over it, blushing. "Now I want wings."

"We brought you some." Natalie held up a bag. "It's double-bagged and still hot. I figured you could eat it on your break."

"I think I'm in love with you."

"You'll always have me. Even if it's only for wings." She winked, and I snorted.

"Thank you. And, yes, I'll always love you for Aiden's wings." I took the bag from her and moaned. I could smell the lemon pepper, teriyaki, and barbecue sauce and nearly groaned.

"You guys got my favorites."

"Of course. And we told Aiden that they were for

you, so he made them extra special." Mackenzie winked.

I rolled my eyes. "Dillon's brother doesn't know how to make anything that's *not* special."

Elise nodded. "That is true. He's working on a few recipes for the new restaurant, so he's busier than ever these days. Of course, I feel like Dillon's just as busy."

"Pacey, too." Mackenzie searched through the teen section next to us, a slight frown on her face. "He has a couple of upcoming projects. We're all a little stressed out."

"Pacey can handle it. He's good at juggling things." Mackenzie gave me a weird look, and I cringed. "I meant with work. Not friends or anything like that. Sorry, did that come out weird?" I asked.

Mackenzie shook her head. "No, I'm the one who's acting weird. Ignore me. I've had a long day."

"Tell me about it," Natalie said, rubbing her shoulders. I knew she was trying to help me since I kept acting strangely around Mackenzie, and I appreciated it. "A seriously long day over here, too. Anyway, we just wanted to stop by. And I want to hear about your date with Xander. You went back to your room right after, so we didn't get to talk. Did it go okay?" Natalie asked.

I returned to shelving, looking around for any customers. Things were slower in this section, so I had a few moments to come up with an answer. "It was good. Nice."

My roommates winced. "*Nice*?" Elise prodded.

"Nice as in comfortable. It wasn't horrible. He's a good guy. A nice guy."

"*Nice guy* in air quotes?" Mackenzie asked.

I shook my head. "No, not like that. At least, I don't think so. He was just...okay. Not demanding."

"Are you going out with him again?" Natalie asked.

I nodded. "That's the plan. However, I don't have much time for dating because of school, writing, work, and just…everything. It's a lot."

"I know it is," Natalie said as she squeezed my hand. "If you need anything, we're here."

I smiled at my friends. "I know. And I'm grateful. Now, I need to get back to work and then deal with my homework. Thank you for the wings. They will get me through the night."

"We're always here for you," Mackenzie said as she leaned down and kissed my cheek.

I smiled up at her. "You are all pretty amazing."

"Go work, play with your men. I'll be home a bit later."

"Sounds like a plan," Elise said, clapping her hands. "Not the man part because they're all busy, but we still have homework and lives without them."

"Yes, especially those without boyfriends. It would

be nice if we stopped putting that in all of our schedules," Natalie said, rolling her eyes.

I laughed as they left, shaking my head. My phone buzzed, and I pulled it out of my pocket once again.

Dad: *Do you think you can come over after work? Or will it be too late?*

Alarm shot up my spine. I quickly texted back.

Me: *Is everything okay?*

Dad: *Yes. If it were an emergency, I would have called you. Promise. I just have a few things to look over. I could use your eyes.*

Worry gnawed at me, and I bit my lip.

Me: *I'll be over right after work.*

It would be a long night, but that didn't matter. My dad needed me. Of course, I would be there.

Anxiety ran through me for the rest of the evening as I rang up a few more customers and worked on more stocking. By the time I was done and everything was locked up for the night, I was tired but wired. I needed to know what was wrong and what my dad needed. I was exhausted yet nervous at the same time. I didn't know what my dad might tell me, but I knew it likely wouldn't be good. Not if he wanted me to come to my childhood home so late in the day after work when I had classes in the morning.

I parked in the driveway and made my way inside, using the key as I always did. Dad had said that this was my home, even if I didn't live here anymore. I wasn't sure if I would ever be able to call this *home* again. Not when I walked inside and only thought about my mom, of her being sick and how quickly cancer had taken her. We hadn't had time to adjust to her being sick before she was gone. One day, she was a little tired. The next day, she was no longer on this Earth. And it felt as if I couldn't catch up. Calling this *home* only made it worse.

"Nessa?" Dad asked from the kitchen as I walked in.

"It's me. At least, you'd better hope it's me, considering I used the key." I tried to keep my voice light. I felt anything *but* light deep inside.

I locked up, set my bag on the table next to the front door, and looked around the home that had helped to raise me. Everything had a layer of dust, and my dad's armchair looked to be the only place anyone had sat recently. Mom's touches were still on everything, and I knew that my dad wouldn't change anything, no matter what.

I'd have to come over someday and help him clean, but I didn't have time tonight. Sadly, we couldn't afford a maid or anyone to come and help him. It was only the two of us alone in the world now. I wasn't sure what that meant or what I was supposed to do about it.

"Hey, Daddy," I said as I kissed his cheek. He was

at the kitchen table, his wire-rimmed glasses falling down his nose as he looked up at me. He had a cup of black coffee next to his elbow and papers strewn about the table, his laptop next to him.

"Hey, Nessa baby."

I looked at the bills on the surface, the spreadsheet on the screen, and swallowed hard. "Things are rough, aren't they?" I asked.

"Why don't you take a seat? Do you want some coffee?"

"It's too late for coffee for me. And probably for you. How old is this stuff?" I asked as I sniffed the mug and winced.

"Old enough. But waste not, want not and all that." He didn't take a drink. Instead, he leaned back in the chair and rubbed his temples.

"How bad is it?" I asked. "I'm not a kid anymore. Don't sugarcoat it."

He met my gaze and nodded. "Fine, we're broke. We're going to be broke for a long time. The insurance paid for some of Mom's things, but not everything. We had decent life insurance, but while it covered the cremation and initial costs, and my job pays for the mortgage for now as well as a few of our outstanding bills, it can't cover everything."

"By *everything*, you mean school." Tension rode me, and I fisted my hands in front of me. "I have a semester and a half left and have a scholarship for part of it. Plus, I have loans. But is that enough?"

"It should be. You don't need to worry about that. We'll get you through school. I promise."

I shook my head. "You say that, but I'm not sure. I know I have a year's worth of school left in terms of bills and loans, but you can use my college fund if you need it."

He shook his head. "No, I didn't ask you here for you to give me the money your mother and I saved for you. The money that *you* saved for school. You need that for your future. Your sheepskin to ride with the flock and find out who you need to be."

"I don't know, Dad."

"It's fine. We're not going to lose the house."

My eyes widened. "We could lose the house?"

"I just said we wouldn't." I knew he was lying. It was written all over his face. Both of my parents had decent jobs, but we were lower middle class at best. When Mom died, Dad's job should have been good enough, but insurance took so much out of us. School was expensive, and medical bills for Mom on top of my dad's health issues meant we'd wiped out any savings accounts they had.

"If you're saying that, it means you had to think about it."

"I'm doing okay, Nessa. We both are. As long as you get a job outside of college, you should be fine."

"I don't know what I'm doing, Dad."

"I love you. I know you were supposed to have time to figure out your next steps, but you're going to need to think about it now. You only have a year left. Figuring out your path is never easy, and it'll only be more complicated now."

"I don't know. Maybe I could take fewer courses and get some money back."

"Nessa," my dad warned.

"A degree from a community college is as good as a university. Maybe I can do that for the last year," I said, even as my stomach turned. I had worked so hard for everything, but the loans were expensive, and I didn't even qualify for everything. There were only so many scholarships out there for an English major, and I knew I would have to go to grad school if I wanted to continue my path. I couldn't afford that.

I couldn't afford anything, it seemed. The stress on my dad just then? I didn't know if me finishing school like this was worth it.

"You're not going to drop out. You're going to finish. We'll make it work."

I saw the uncertainty in his gaze, and I knew all of my wishes and hard work might not be enough. We were so close, but it might not be enough.

Just like before, *I* wasn't enough. I never was. I would have to change something. Fix something. Only I didn't know what or how to do it. My dad was floundering, and I was treading water right next to him. My mom was gone, and we couldn't lie in stasis forever. I didn't know how to fix anything. Didn't know how to make any of this better.

Dropping out this semester would save enough money to keep us afloat for now. It wasn't like my major did much. I had gone to school for a dream. However, it seemed that even though I'd had a plan, a way to continue my future, it wouldn't be enough.

Another choice I had made was about to blow up in my face. Only this time, it would hurt my dad, too. And I only had myself to blame.

Four

Miles

I should have known it was a dream the moment Nessa wrapped her hand around my cock, but I didn't. Instead, I let myself believe that it was real because dream Nessa liked me. Dream Nessa said she wanted to be with me. And dream Nessa was currently licking down my Adonis line and nipping at my skin. I groaned, sliding my hand through her hair as she slowly lapped at the side of my dick before sucking the tip. With that motion, my body shook as I neared release. Only this was a dream, and my body somehow kept going as if it knew that it needed to hold on just a bit longer. Dream Nessa's mouth was damned talented, but I needed to be stronger. I was not about to blow on the first lick and touch.

Nessa sucked me down again, and I pulled at her hair, needing her mouth. I just needed her. At this moment, it wasn't a dream for me. This was real. It was her wanting to be with me. And it wasn't only in my imagination because, hell, I was dream Miles at the moment, too. She crawled up my body, and I moaned, taking her mouth, delving my tongue between her lips. She whimpered, and I cupped her breasts, her nipples hard little nubs against my palms. I keened, needing more. Needing everything.

I reached for her, wanting her on top of me. She looked up at me, pushing her hair back from her face as she straddled me, and then she winked before her eyes widened slightly and…she was gone.

I was eighteen again, sitting in a car, my mouth open in a scream, two steps behind once more.

I wouldn't be able to stop this. I looked over as Rachelle smiled at me, that loopy grin that told me she'd had one too many drinks. But then again, how was I supposed to know? I'd never drunk before. The first night I did, my twin sister had gotten behind the wheel. We should have done something. I should have made better choices, but I hadn't. I knew what came next. This wasn't a dream. It was a memory. Rachelle looked at me again, and then there were screams, shouts that echoed and would never go away. Mine, hers, my family's. Everyone's.

The car hit metal, and there was no going back. Rachelle looked at me again, but I didn't know how. She gave me a sad smile, opened her mouth to say something, and then there was nothing.

"Miles, wake up," Tanner said as he shook me awake. I lay hunched over my books at my desk and groaned as I sat back, fixing my glasses that were now askew on my face.

"Shit, did I fall asleep?" I asked the obvious question.

Tanner gave me a weird look. "Yes. We had a long week." A pause. "You okay?"

From the way he looked at me, I knew I must've said something in my sleep. Maybe screamed my sister's name again.

The others weren't aware of what lurked in my nightmares. All of us kept secrets, and that was fine with me. They didn't need to know that the first time I'd ever had a drink, I had decided to let my twin drive, even though she'd had more. I'd been too drunk to rationalize anything at the time.

Rachelle had always been the partier. The one who

got busted for weed and booze when we were fourteen. I had tried to take the rap for her then, hating the disappointed looks on my parents' faces, but they had known. They always knew that I was the *good son*. The geeky one, who wore glasses and did well in school and never partied because I was too afraid to get caught. At high school graduation, I had wanted to let loose, to prove that I wasn't that person anymore.

Only I had made stupid decisions because my best friend, my twin, had told me that everything was fine, that she could handle it—that she did it all the time. Drunk me had known not to trust her but hadn't been in the right frame of mind to do anything about it. Sober me never would have done that. I hadn't made the right decision.

And now, Rachelle was gone.

Nobody else needed to know that. Not when it hurt so much to think about it.

"Shit, did I drool on my books?" I tried to alleviate some of the tension, but I knew it wouldn't work.

Tanner just gave me a look but didn't ask. For that, I was grateful. Then again, I didn't ask questions about his past, either. We were roommates, and he was my closest friend out of the four of us—five if you included our former roommate, Sanders.

"You doing okay?" Tanner asked.

I shrugged off the question. "Yes, just studying hard and all that."

He blinked. "If you want to talk about it…"

I shook my head quickly. "No, I'm fine. Thanks, though."

Tanner just frowned before shrugging and making his way to the door. "We're having dinner and drinks. Pacey wanted to make sure you were coming. He knows how much you like cheese."

I smiled at that as I closed my books and wiped at my face in case I'd actually drooled. "You know me and cheese," I said and laughed.

"You're almost as bad as Dillon."

"What am I bad at?" Dillon asked as we walked into the kitchen. Pacey had indeed made a large cheese board with crackers, bread, and fruits. Dillon stood at the massive stove, stirring something in a large pot.

I sniffed and smiled. "Is that Aiden's chili?" I asked.

My roommate raised a brow. "No, it's *my* chili using Aiden's recipe."

"Considering you wanted to be a chef, it's probably just as good as Aiden's," I said, as I leaned over the pot to get another whiff.

Dillon rolled his eyes. "Let's not tell Aiden that. He'll only want to one-up me."

"That means we'd get to taste the offerings of the

challenge. You guys are brothers. It's what you do," Pacey said with a shrug.

A small smile played on Dillon's lips. "Yes, we are."

I knew Aiden hadn't been in Dillon's life for long, so the whole dynamic between the brothers was still pretty new. That thought only made me miss Rachelle more. After all, she had been my twin. My best friend. The person who had known me better than anyone. Now, she was gone. Damn, I needed to get her out of my mind.

I cleared my throat. "Are we eating in here?"

"No, let's go to the living room. I already got the beers out." Tanner tilted his head toward the door and picked up a bowl from the counter.

I nodded. "I'm starving."

Pacey leaned forward over the kitchen island. "I'll get the cheeseboard out to the living room, but you guys try not to make a mess."

"We won't hurt your fancy fucking furniture," Tanner said with a laugh, and I grinned when Pacey flipped him off. We were all past the initial awkward roommate stage. Now, we were friends—even if we liked to give each other shit.

"How's school going?" Pacey asked the group as we all sat down and dove into our chili and cheese board.

"We're going to have this discussion?" Tanner dug into his meal with gusto.

"What? It's a legitimate question." Pacey frowned.

Tanner rolled his eyes. "Fine, classes are fine. I'm nearing my first set of exams, and I'm not excited about them, but we're getting there."

"You're still doing grad school after, right?" Dillon asked as he took a chip. "I mean, I have business school, and I still want to take a few culinary classes to make sure I'm ready to help Aiden when the time comes, but I think almost all of us have grad school of some sort afterward."

Tanner sighed. "Yes. Though I don't like thinking about the cost."

I held back a groan as I cringed. "I hate that school is getting so ridiculous these days." I finished my bowl of chili and thought about getting another one as I licked my lips. "I'm limited to what schools I can go to because they have larger programs that are *publish or perish*, even though I don't want to be in academia when I'm done with school."

"You're going to need your doctorate to even hit the industry you want?" Tanner asked.

"For the pay that I want, yes. I can find schools that will work for that, and many people in my field only get their master's, but I want the doctorate."

I could feel my cheeks redden as Dillon grinned. "You want us to call you Dr. Miles?"

"It'd be Dr. Fraser," Pacey corrected with a laugh.

My face heated even more. "Please, don't call me that."

"I'm sure if you ever get a girlfriend, you could play doctor quite nicely," Tanner quipped, and I flipped him off.

"Hey, don't make fun of the guy just because he doesn't have a girlfriend," Pacey warned, the light in his eyes dancing.

"I hate all of you." I laughed.

"You don't." Pacey grinned.

Dillon leaned back in his chair. "You love us."

"Not really," I said, shaking my head again. I made a plate of various cheeses and nearly gorged myself. "I don't have time for a girlfriend. Frankly, I don't know how so many of you guys do have time for girlfriends." I gave Tanner a pointed look. "Or boyfriends."

"I'm not saying a poly relationship is easy, but it's doable. As long as it's the suitable poly."

"As in don't add extra connections to the relationship?" Pacey asked dryly.

"Pretty much," Tanner grumbled. "I mean, you can't call it monogamous because you're with more than one person, but not cheating would be a wonderful fucking thing, don't you think?" Tanner scowled into his beer.

I frowned, wondering why he was growling so much about it. He hadn't seemed too hurt about the relationship ending when it happened, but maybe I'd been wrong.

"I'm sorry," Dillon said softly. "We didn't mean to bring all that up."

Tanner shook his head. "No, it's fine. Their new foursome broke up anyway. Now, they're all on the prowl and texting." His phone dinged, and he narrowed his eyes at it. "And continuing to text me."

"You should just block the number." I leaned forward, trying to come up with a solution.

Tanner shook his head. "No. Because if there's an actual emergency and they need help, I'll be there."

My eyes widened. "Wow."

My roommate snorted. "Don't *wow* me. They don't have any other family. They're the people they each have to lean on. I don't want to be the asshole who lets them die in a ditch because I'm pissed off. Yet, I also don't want to fuck them anymore. There's a balance."

That made me laugh. "A good balance."

"What about you and that girl? The one from your classes?" Pacey asked.

I shook my head as I leaned into the couch, my beer resting on my thigh. "Not happening. She's with one of the other girls in our classes now."

"Aww. Broke your heart?" Tanner asked.

I snorted. "Not even close. I don't even think she

liked me. She just wanted to make sure she could blow me and beat me in the curve."

That made Dillon and Pacey both snort and nearly drop their beers.

"I don't know why, but I did not expect that sentence to come out of your mouth," Dillon said, shaking his head.

"What? She wanted my dick and told me point blank that she wanted it because I beat her on the curve. And, guess what? I'm *still* going to beat her on the fucking curve, but she won't get anywhere near my dick."

"I hear nobody's getting near your dick," Tanner teased.

"Keep talking about my dick, and I'm going to assume you want it," I taunted, surprising myself.

Tanner gave me a brief look before throwing his head back with a laugh. "Okay, you win. And, no, I don't want your dick. Sorry."

"It's fine. I'll just have to deal with the emotional turmoil that comes from you not wanting me that way. I'll be strong and deal with the grief. But I will find a way. I will persevere," I said, clapping my hands to each syllable. At this point, Dillon and Pacey were laughing so hard they were nearly bent over the couch. I shook my head. "If you think I'm that hysterical, we're clearly on bean and cheese overload."

"I don't know. You have a little pep in your step," Pacey said.

"Pep in his step?" Dillon asked, laughing again.

"What? It's a saying."

"I don't think it's a current British *or* American saying. It's more of a 1950s' saying," Tanner corrected.

Pacey scowled. "Oh, fuck all y'all."

"Did the British guy just say y'all?" I asked, laughing harder.

"What? It was in a show Mackenzie was watching. Now, I can't stop saying it. Do you have any idea how hard it is to stop saying y'all, even with this accent?" Pacey asked. My side hurt, but we kept eating, drinking, and laughing.

Yes, I had homework to do. Yes, I probably needed to stop dreaming about Nessa. But I didn't care. We needed this time, and I would take it.

When we cleaned up and went to our respective work areas to get some homework done, I looked over at Tanner and shook my head.

"What's that for?" my roommate asked as he sat down behind his desk.

"I'm just thinking about how while Pacey and Dillon are decently similar, you and I are nothing alike. I don't even think you would be my friend if we weren't roommates." I cringed. "Maybe those three beers are making me say way too many things I shouldn't."

Tanner gave me a look and shook his head. "I'd still be your friend, but that would mean you'd have to talk to me to make it happen. I'm not some big, popular guy, Miles. I'm just an asshole who doesn't like people. One who gets into shitty relationships and fucks things up. I think you're the one who's too good for me."

"Really? You think that? I'm the guy who can't even talk to people because the one person I *could* talk to is dead," I said and shut my mouth.

Tanner's eyes widened. "Miles?" he asked, his voice low.

"No. I don't want to talk about it. I shouldn't have… I just… I'm fine."

"Are you?" he asked softly.

My heart twisted, and I ignored the pain. "I am. Sorry. Just a long night."

"Miles."

"No, it's nothing. Really. I'm just feeling shitty. Maybe I need to get laid."

"That could be part of it, but that's not all of it." Tanner's voice was so low, I'd almost missed the words.

"I don't want a heart-to-heart. Is that okay?" I swallowed hard, my throat tight.

"I am the last person who will ever force you to

have a heart-to-heart. But if you want to talk, I'm here."

"I know." I looked him directly in the eyes. "I don't want to talk. I've done all the talking I want to do. Apparently, drinking makes me fuck up. Again."

The chili and the cheese in my stomach started to curdle, and I nearly threw up. I'd had way more than three beers when I was in the car with Rachelle. I'd had so much fucking liquor that they'd had to pump my stomach. I wasn't drunk tonight. I was just tired and fucking up once again.

I hated myself a little, but there weren't any words to make it better. I packed my stuff and went to my bedroom, my stomach roiling. I locked the door behind me, then went to my bathroom and promptly threw up everything I had eaten earlier.

I had fucked up before, and my sister had died because of it.

Now, here I was, spouting shit because I was a loser. I couldn't even have a steady relationship—friendship or otherwise—because nobody knew who I was.

I didn't even know who I was. I knew what I wanted to be once I left school, but only in the sense of having a job and a career. I didn't know anything else outside of that. I didn't know what I would do when I had to leave Aaron behind. I didn't know what my parents would do when they couldn't oversee my every action any longer.

It was all twisting in my head, and as I brushed my teeth and lay down on my bed, I couldn't help but wonder why I ever thought I could have a crush on someone like Nessa. She might've had her heart broken, but she had everything together. She knew who she was and was proud of it. I was some asshole who wasn't even good at figuring out what I wanted. The one thing I knew I wanted above all else was to have my sister back—and that was something that would never happen, no matter how hard I wished.

Five

Nessa

"Why am I taking this class again?" I asked as I leaned against the pillow after glaring at the textbook.

Elise slowly slid down the back of the couch to lean her head on my shoulder. "I have no idea. Why do we do this to ourselves? Why can't we be full adults already and not in school anymore? Where we have jobs and lives where we're worried about things other than homework."

I held back a wince because I was afraid if things didn't get better soon, this might be my last semester with them. I only had a couple of weeks before I could no longer get a refund if I dropped out. I wanted to make sure I didn't end up in crippling debt with my dad losing the house, so that I could have a dream I wasn't even sure I wanted anymore.

"If only Pacey and Mackenzie could get that time machine to work."

Elise snorted. "I have a feeling Corinne would have been pushing us to finish our homework right now. That way, we could go out and enjoy ourselves."

I smiled, no longer feeling the sharp pain I used to feel anytime someone mentioned our friend. Corinne had died nearly a year ago now, and I missed her every day. I still couldn't quite believe that she was gone, but it wasn't as if I could go back and change things. I'd learned that the hard way.

"She and Mackenzie would have been best friends because Mackenzie's already done with her work and out on a date with Pacey."

"That sounds wonderful. I wish I was on a date," Elise grumbled, looking through her work.

"With Pacey?" I asked, teasing, and then winced as she gave me a look.

Considering I'd had a massive crush on him and things had gotten awkward between us, I probably shouldn't have brought him up. Yet, here we were, even in his house. We were at the guys' home because our neighbor was installing new windows, and the sound had been driving us batty. Dillon had handed over the keys, kissed Elise soundly on the mouth, and told us to get studying. I was only slightly jealous of the love in his eyes every time he looked at her.

There was something there—sheer happiness. And while I might be a little jealous, I didn't care. They were right for each other. I wanted to find that, too.

"Are you okay?" Elise asked tentatively.

I rolled my eyes, trying to force some cheer into my voice. I didn't love Pacey, but I was still embarrassed that I had fallen so hard. "I'm fine. I didn't mean to bring him up, even though we are in his house. I'm over him," I said, and it didn't feel like a lie. I called that progress.

"Okay, if you say so."

I growled and closed my textbook. There was no way I could focus. "I'm not like that anymore. I don't know what I was thinking before when it came to him, but it's not that anymore. It's not some huge, overwhelming need to be with him. I was silly to even think it was."

"There's nothing silly about having a crush on a guy you respect."

"It is a little silly when you mistake it for love and almost hurt some of the people you care about the most in the process."

Elise shook her head. "You didn't hurt them."

"True. At least, I don't think I did. It doesn't

matter. Mackenzie and Pacey are going strong. They're freaking adorable, and I am slowly getting through school and figuring out my life. I don't have time for guys."

"I thought you had a date with Xander later tonight." Elise raised a brow.

I shrugged. "Maybe I have time to *try* to date, but nothing too serious."

"You don't think Xander's the one?"

I snorted. "He's a nice guy, and maybe we can have some relaxed fun, but I'm not looking for forever. I don't even know what I want for the rest of my life, let alone a forever with a guy."

"Forever at our age can be a pretty long time. Of course, we all know that it sometimes doesn't happen." Her smile turned dreamy, and I knew she likely wasn't even aware of the look on her face.

My heart ached, but I shook my head. "I'm not going to throw myself at anyone just because I'm afraid we're all going to die super young like Corinne did." I winced. "I didn't mean to sound so harsh."

"No, I get it. I don't think I went to Dillon because we lost Corinne."

"No, you pushed him away," I countered, and she sighed.

"Oh, yes, there was that."

"Dillon and I made it through those decisions and

are better than ever for it. And you and Pacey are back to being friends."

"Maybe not as close as we once were, but I can see that. He has so much going on in his life, and he needs time with Mackenzie. And, honestly? I'm still a little embarrassed about the way I acted."

"You shouldn't be. Everybody understands."

"That doesn't help the situation." I snorted. "But, Elise? I'm over him."

"Over who?" Tanner asked as he walked into the house, Miles behind him.

I rolled my eyes and did my best not to look at Miles. I didn't know why; it was just so awkward. Every time I looked at him, I thought about *that* kiss. The one I wasn't supposed to remember. Only I did. Oh, I remembered. However, I wouldn't think about it too hard. If I did, things would get weird again. I'd already let them get strange between Pacey and me. And though we were working our way back to the way things had been, and I was responsible for my feelings, I wouldn't fall for anyone else in this house. Even though I couldn't seem to keep my eyes off his face, or not notice how his glasses kept slipping down his nose. I saw everything about him.

Damn it, what was wrong with me?

Elise answered. "It was me. I was just thinking about you and my crush and how I can't ever stop thinking about you. Dillon and I were wondering what we were going to do about it, but we decided maybe it's best if we don't add you to our relationship," she said dryly.

Tanner just grinned that wicked smile I knew melted others' panties. Not mine, but I could see why some felt that way. "All you have to do is ask, babe. I'll be there for you."

"I hope Dillon never hears of this conversation." Miles shook his head before sinking onto the chair beside me. "Hi, Nessa," he said.

I gave him an awkward little wave. Oh, good, now I'd reached a new pinnacle of the awkwardness that was my life. "Hey," I said.

"Hey," Tanner replied as he slid onto the couch next to Elise. "What are we studying?"

"Horrible, horrible things that aren't even for our majors." She gestured toward the book in front of her and sighed.

"Apparently, we're supposed to be well-rounded or some crap," I added.

Miles just shook his head. "I get that, but I wish there were like home-ec classes for college."

Tanner gave him a weird look, and I straightened.

"What? What do you mean?" I asked.

"I like taking a lot of the liberal arts classes that I wouldn't normally have to. I learn a lot while in them.

While my family taught me how to make a budget, change the oil in my car, and even deal with household items that normally wouldn't be an issue, many people don't have that. I think there should be home-ec for college. Hell, I think home-ec should still be required in high school. But now I'm being weird, so I'm just going to shut up."

I shook my head. "Don't shut up. That is smart. If I were learning something productive, that'd be great. Right now, I'm reading a book on history that I'm pretty sure is just an alternate version and not the truth because it doesn't talk about the atrocities committed."

Miles winced. "That's the epitome of suck, and I'm sorry you have to deal with that."

I shrugged. "It's college. There were only so many options for this semester to fill that requirement. You would think I'd be happy with books. Not so much this time."

"I think I took that class sophomore year." Tanner leaned forward. "Dr. Peterman?"

"Yep. Asshole."

"He is, and he hates women," Tanner said.

I sighed. "Oh, I know. Thankfully, the class isn't graded on a curve with participation, or I would probably end up with a C just because he feels like it."

"Only one more year of school." Miles paused.

"And then, all of our grad schools and everything else with that. However, one more year of *this* school."

"Yay," Elise added deadpan. "With that, I need to go. I told Dillon that I would meet him at the bar. I'll finish up my work there."

"He doing okay?" I asked.

Elise grinned. "He's doing great. He has a paper due tomorrow, and one of his nieces has a cold so everybody's working overtime trying to get both restaurants set up and everything. It's a lot. And while his brothers are trying to push Dillon not to work as hard as he has been, it's Dillon. Of course, he wants to help his family."

"It's nice that he has them," I said honestly.

"I know. Dillon will finish his paper, and I'm going to drive him home after he closes. It's just going to be a long day."

"Let me know if you need anything."

Elise grinned at me. "I'm not going to need anything from you. You have a date."

Tanner grinned at me as Miles leaned forward. "You have a date?" he asked. I did my best not to look deeper into his words. I had kissed him when I was drunk. He didn't kiss me back. I didn't need to think about him in any other way now.

"Yes, I do."

"Going to get lucky?" Tanner asked.

I threw a crumpled-up piece of paper at him. "Gross."

"If it's gross, you're not doing it right," Tanner said.

"Whatever." I shook my head as Tanner and Elise began packing up and heading out. Miles held his phone, staring at something, seemingly in his own world.

Tanner went up to his room, scowling at his phone as he did, and Elise headed towards Dillon's. That left me on the couch, picking up my things as Miles scrolled through something on his cell.

"Nessa, I forgot I had something to show you." Miles' words pulled me out of my thoughts.

"Oh?" Why were things so awkward when it came to him?

"You were looking for that book on Jane Austen, right?"

"I'm always looking for books on Jane Austen," I answered with a laugh.

"True, but there was a biography you wanted to read in paperback. The one that's out of print?"

"Oh, yes! Why?"

"I think I found a copy. At least, I believe so. It's in the library. Come on."

He stood, and my heart raced, though I wasn't sure if it was only about the book.

"You found it?"

"I think it came with the house. I was bored one day, looking through all the books. It might not be the same one, though. I left it where it was so I didn't accidentally lose it in my room or something."

"I would hate to have to search your room to find it if that were the case."

I swallowed hard as both of us gave each other looks. I tried not to read too much into it.

"Here. I think I remember it over here."

I stood next to him in the library as he slowly reached for the book. He was so close to me and smelled so good. I swallowed hard, attempting not to think about it. I tried not to look at him because I didn't want him knowing that I was thinking about him or trying *not* to look at him.

What was wrong with me? The tension was palpable, and I swore I could hear every breath he took. I felt the warmth of his body next to mine.

My hair stood on end, and I wanted to reach out. To brush his skin and see what he felt like. But I didn't.

I wasn't going to lose my mind and fall for another guy in this house.

He finally cleared his throat. If it were any more awkward or steamier between us, his glasses would have fogged up—or I'd trip over myself.

"Here you go," he said as he handed me the book.

Our fingertips brushed, and I swallowed hard before I pulled back.

"This is it. Thank you." I wanted to reach up and kiss his cheek like I would have any other day to say thank you because that's who I was. But I didn't.

Instead, I met his gaze, and my eyes moved to his lips. I stopped myself.

I had to.

Miles pulled away first, and I hated that I hadn't. "I need to go work on my homework in my room. I need to focus."

"Good. I have a date."

"I remember."

"Oh. Right." I was annoyed that I'd even brought it up.

"With that guy. Xander? Things are going pretty well between the two of you?" he added, sticking his hands into his pockets.

I didn't want to read too much into his words or tone. He didn't like me like that. He hadn't mentioned the kiss, and I hadn't either. I just saw too much tension in everything we did these days.

"I don't know about that," I said honestly. "It's just a date. Dinner. I need to eat." Could I sound any lamer?

"Have fun, stay safe."

"Always. And thank you for the book. Really, thank you."

"Anything, Nessa."

His gaze met mine again, and then he shrugged and walked away, leaving me standing there as if I were losing my mind.

And in a home I didn't own, acting the fool.

I quickly put the book with my stuff, being careful not to hurt the pages. It was Pacey's book. Or the house's, anyway. I wasn't sure how it had even gotten here. I would read it, though. Then, I would return it.

And do my best not to think about Miles the entire time.

I stuffed everything into my bag and headed back to my house. The neighbors were still banging on the windows, the installation taking forever. Our house was empty when I walked in. I quickly changed into tights and a dress that went to my knees and slid my feet into flats. It was a cute outfit, nothing sexy because I wasn't going for seductive. We were going to a small restaurant that was similar to the diner we had been to before. Nothing fancy, just a night out. With a nice guy.

One who did absolutely nothing for me. But I wasn't going to think about that.

I redid my makeup and told myself that this was for the best. I was trying to find time to relax, even though I couldn't. I had to work the next day, and I had classes that would exhaust me, but I would still pretend that me taking time for myself like this was worth it.

Only I wasn't sure that Xander *was*.

By the time I made it to the restaurant, Xander was already there, a Diet Coke and water at my place. He had ordered for me. While I appreciated it, it was a little weird. I didn't always want Diet Coke, but I wouldn't say anything. Xander was *nice.*

"Nessa," he said as he stood and kissed my cheek. I smiled, holding back a cringe. I hadn't enjoyed the kiss we'd shared before, and now that I thought about it, I hadn't exactly enjoyed any of the time we'd been together, either. It had been a moment in time and could have been with anyone. I really needed to try harder.

"Hi." I sat, and Xander smiled at me. I knew this would be the last date I would go on with him.

He just wasn't for me. And, frankly, I had enough on my plate. I tried. I wasn't even thinking about Pacey anymore. I was over him and had figured I'd set him on a pedestal in my mind when I hadn't needed to.

Now, I needed to get over this thing with Miles. Once I did, I would be fine. I had way more important things to worry about than who I was going to date in my final year of school.

I pushed all worries from my mind and did my best

to enjoy my date, even as I told myself I wouldn't do this again.

Xander was likable, but he wasn't for me.

I was starting to think nobody was. And maybe that was for the best.

Six

Miles

"We can do this. It's just garlic, right?" Natalie asked, and I laughed.

"You say that, and yet I thought garlic was that powdery stuff you sprinkle on things."

"We shouldn't say that around Dillon. He would never forgive us."

I laughed and shook my head as Natalie did her best to peel the skin from the clove. We had YouTube up and cookbooks surrounding us as we tried our best to cook.

When the two of us realized we were the worst cooks of the group, we had decided to learn how to do the basics. If we'd had the time, we would have taken a class. But for now, the internet was teaching us, and we wouldn't let Dillon or the others know that we had no idea what we were doing.

"How am I getting garlic everywhere? And I think I had a cut on my hand, and now the garlic juice is burning me. Why did we say we wanted to cook again?" Natalie asked, her voice slightly below panic level.

I winced before I took off my glasses and tried to rub my eyes with my forearm. "Why am I wearing my glasses when I know not to when cutting onions? The fumes are just getting trapped under there, and I'm dying."

Natalie started to laugh, and I flipped her off.

"And they say you're the nice one," she teased.

"You're supposed to be the nice one, too, yet still you mock my pain." I went to the sink, took off my glasses, and tossed water on my face after washing my hands.

"We are the worst at this. We don't even have the oven on yet."

I froze. "Were we supposed to preheat it? I thought this was just a pan on the stove."

"I don't know. What do the instructions say?"

"I don't know, either. You're the one with the recipe," I shot back.

She shook her head. "I thought you were the one who found this one."

"No, that was you." I paused. "Wait. What are we making?"

"A version of chicken cacciatore, but I don't think we're doing it right. I'm just glad we're the only ones who'll be eating it. Are you sure Dillon and Pacey said they were taking the girls out for a double date?" she asked.

I nodded. "Yes. And Nessa is at work, same with Tanner. So, it's just us." I paused. "Not that this is a date or anything."

She gave me a look and shook her head. "Stop. We're just friends, and I'm fine with that."

"Oh, thank God," I said. "We already know I'm awkward as hell. I'd probably be worse if I thought the two of us were dating."

"I'm not sure exactly how to take that," she said with a laugh.

I cringed. "Not that you aren't wonderful..." I began, and she shook her head.

"You should stop while you're ahead."

"I can't stop in the middle of a thought like that. I like you as a friend."

"Same. Not that you aren't adorable." She winked.

"Great. *Adorable.* That's exactly what I want to hear." I smiled as I said it, and she laughed.

We went back to cooking, and soon, I cleared my throat. "So, I was right in remembering Nessa is working today?" I asked, trying to act happy.

Natalie gave me a bland stare. "Yes, Nessa is working. However, I don't know when she's off. She could be here at any moment. Do you need to go freshen up before she shows up?"

I blushed as I put my glasses back on. "No. It's not like that between us."

"And are you sad about that?" she asked.

"No, Nessa isn't for me. I know that. She had a crush on Pacey."

Natalie studied my face. "And that is completely over. I don't think it's going to work out with that Xander guy, either."

I perked up, meeting her gaze. "Really?" I asked, annoyed that I sounded so eager.

She gave me a knowing smile. "She told me that it wasn't, so I'm going with that."

I set that aside since I didn't want to focus too hard on what it could mean. And the best defense is the best offense. Or something sports-related. "Since you and I will never work out…" I teased. "Do you have your eye on anyone else?" I asked, trying not to think about Nessa since I was already acting weird enough.

Natalie shrugged. "Not really. I'm not so good at the whole dating thing. Or the talking to guys thing."

I blinked at her, then looked down at myself. "Um, is there something you need to know about me?" I asked, only half teasing.

She rolled her eyes. "I'm not going to say you're not a guy, but you're nice."

"And guys aren't nice..."

"That's not what I mean. I don't know. The guys at the house treat me like I'm human, don't ignore me, but also don't make me feel weird." She fluttered her hands. "I'm not saying this right."

"The guys are nice." I paused and smiled. "Well, perhaps not Tanner."

"Tanner's nice sometimes." She shrugged before sticking out her tongue, her focus on the garlic she was now carefully trying to mince. "He annoys me, yet I feel like I can talk to him. Just like I can talk to you. You treat me like I'm normal and human, not like this weird little virgin girl who's never actually talked to a guy." She closed her eyes. "I can't believe I just said that out loud."

I winced. "You being a virgin isn't exactly a secret to the eight of us. I mean, Corinne used to mention it offhandedly, and we all heard it."

"Ugh. Just bury me in the backyard right now," she said dryly. "Maybe that's why you guys act like it's not a big deal. Because it's not a big deal. However, I don't know how to say that I'm friends with you all because there's no romantic interest there. Sanders was always an asshole, so I never felt comfortable around him. Tanner annoys the hell out of me, so I'm not usually comfortable when it comes to him, either—except the times when he's kind. The rest of you, however? You are all nice. I like being your friend."

"I like being your friend, too."

She smiled at me just as Nessa walked into the kitchen, her gaze darting between us. "I'm sorry, I didn't know you guys were in here. I'm sorry for interrupting." She turned on her heel, and Natalie just laughed.

"You caught us. So much for trying to keep it a secret, Miles. But I can't."

My eyes widened. "Natalie," I muttered.

"Caught you at what?" Nessa asked cautiously.

Natalie smiled, and it lit up her entire face. "Trying to cook. And not well. We don't even have the stove on, nor do we know where the olive oil is. We're trying to learn."

Nessa turned and smiled at us. "That's so sweet. You two are the worst cooks out of all of us. And that's saying something since I'm not that great."

I scowled. "I'm not *that* bad."

"You are," Nessa said as she came to stand between us. "Are you trying to mince garlic? It's easier when you flatten it with the side of a knife first."

"That's a big knife. What if I cut myself?" Natalie asked.

I nodded. "Dillon showed me that once. I was pretty sure he was about to cut off his whole hand. He's just so quick at it."

"A chef from a Michelin-starred kitchen taught him. He's quick *and* efficient." Nessa shook her head. "Do you want me to help you guys?"

Natalie sighed. "I would say yes, but I know you have work to do. And this is what Miles and I are trying to learn. We need to be able to contribute to our community."

"Or get good at ordering in. Not that I have the funds for that."

Natalie shrugged. "I do. I am great at ordering in, and catering, and the perfect place setting. That's what my family does, after all," she mumbled. My eyebrows went up, but Nessa met my gaze and shook her head. So, we weren't going to talk about that. "Anyway, we were trying to make chicken cacciatore. Or at least a version of it that I found on the internet. Only I'm pretty sure we're only going to give everybody food poisoning if they eat the leftovers."

"I can help if you want," Nessa said, and I looked between the two of them, wondering how I was supposed to deal with this. Every time Nessa entered the room, my cock got hard. It was a little difficult to concentrate and not cut off my fingers or burn myself while cooking, given my dick was so hard I could barely breathe or function.

I'd reached a new low.

"Nessa might be right. We *might* be the worst at this."

Natalie nodded. "Yes, so bad in fact, we can never let Dillon or Tanner know that I'm pretty sure I scalded a pot while boiling water."

"You did what?" Tanner asked.

I turned. "How the hell did you get in here?" I inquired, frowning.

"The back door was unlocked and open," Tanner said, glaring at Natalie. "I thought you said you were going to keep everything locked."

My gaze shot between them, and Natalie raised her chin. "I thought I had. I didn't realize it was open." She paused, her expression falling. "It was open?"

Tanner scowled. "The wind must have gotten it. I'll work on the mechanism. I think it's the lock's issue, not yours."

"Look at that. Tanner saying that it couldn't be my fault and that it could be something else," Natalie singsonged as she went back to cooking.

"Watch it," he grumbled, met my gaze, and then lifted his chin before walking out the door.

I met Nessa's gaze. She shook her head, her eyes wide. "Okay, then."

"Why is Tanner here?" I asked slowly.

"I have no idea," Natalie said. "He texted earlier and said he was coming over to work on something around the house. Mostly because our landlord doesn't do anything, and he's handy." She blushed. "You know what I mean. Not in that way. I don't… We are not like that."

I met Nessa's gaze again. "I believe that," Nessa said, laughing. "Not with how the two of you never seem to get along."

"I was *just* telling Miles that we *do* get along. Though not always. Whatever. I suck at this." She set down the knife. "I don't know what I'm doing." She picked up her phone and stomped out of the kitchen, and I heard Tanner growling about something. She growled right back.

Nessa walked to my side, her eyes even wider. "Is there something going on?" she whispered.

"Between Natalie and me? Hell, no." I winced. "I mean…no. We're just friends."

"That's good. That's what I assumed," Nessa said slowly. "But I meant between Tanner and Natalie."

I shrugged, embarrassed. "I have no idea. I wouldn't have thought so until just now. Wow."

"Exactly. *Wow.*" She swallowed hard and rocked

back on her feet. "Anyway, do you want help cooking? I guess this is dinner? I mean...if I'm invited."

I looked around at the messy kitchen and the fact that we hadn't even started cooking beyond the prep. "This was *supposed* to be dinner. Only I don't even know when we're going to be able to eat."

"Come on. I'll help you."

I shook my head. "I thought you were working today."

"I was. I did my shift and then thought I would come home and try to get some work done. So, here I am. And I will. But let me help you cook first."

"You don't have to. I can figure it out."

She raised a brow.

"I can," I growled.

"I'm sure you can. Still, let me help you. I'm good at this. Decent, anyway. And I know this recipe." Nessa tapped the screen. "Let me help you."

"I'd appreciate it. Are you going to need help with your homework? Anything I can do?"

She straightened. "Actually, yes. I'm in a stupid statistics class, and it's kicking my ass."

"Ah, that *other* class you kept putting off."

"Yes. I hate it. I vaguely remember when we were signing up, and you said you were decent at it."

"It's not exactly my major, but I took the class. I can help if you want."

"I'd be grateful. I'd rather just keep writing."

"Writing? For work? School? Or the book you're working on?"

Her gaze shot to mine. "You know I'm writing a book?"

I shrugged, trying to act nonchalant. "Maybe."

"Miles," she teased as she deftly minced the garlic and chopped the onion. How could someone do that so quickly?

"I overheard you and the girls talking about it while working at my desk. The house is loud sometimes. I didn't mean to eavesdrop. It just sort of happened."

"Serves me right for actually speaking it out loud in the living room rather than from behind a tightly closed door with a lock in a soundproof room." She shook her head, a smile playing on her lips. "Let me show you how to cut these tomatoes."

I tilted my head, studying her face. "Can't you just buy the canned ones?"

"Yes, but you didn't. You bought tomatoes, meaning we're going to have to cook them down. We can do this, Miles."

"Maybe I should have started with just mashed potatoes. Or steak. I can grill a steak."

"As can any guy I know, according to the laws of being a man or whatever other patriarchal society thing is out there."

"That was a nice segue," I said, laughing.

"I had a rough day. Too many customers searching through our books then going to their phone and ordering online from the big online store that will not be named."

I went still. "Seriously?"

"Yep. And they didn't even bother hiding it. They just buy their print books, not even ebooks, even though they're holding the book in their hands. I don't get it. However, there's nothing I can do other than curse them behind their backs and maybe make a voodoo doll or something. You know, I'm not in the mood to do that."

"It seems like a lot of work and responsibility."

She grinned. "Exactly. Let's get through this. While it simmers, we can work on statistics."

She turned, ran into my chest, and put her hands on my abs. I reached out to steady her, my hands on her hips, and did my best not to let them move around to cup her ass.

She was just…right there, her breasts pressed against me. I nearly groaned.

"Oh," she whispered, swallowing hard.

"Sorry. You okay?"

"Yes, I think I am," she breathed.

My gaze moved to her lips, and I swallowed hard. I wanted to kiss her, wanted to do something. Instead, I just stood there. But I didn't move back, didn't do anything.

She looked up at me, her mouth parted. It'd be so easy to lower my head and brush my lips across hers. But I didn't. I didn't want to ruin things. The problem was, I could so easily do that.

"I shouldn't do this," she whispered, and I nodded before I pulled away, feeling cold at the sudden lack of her touch.

She rubbed her palms on her thighs and swallowed hard. "I'm just…I don't want to ruin what we have, Miles."

I met her gaze and nodded. "Same here. You're my friend, Nessa. Sometimes, I feel like I don't have a lot of those."

"You're such a nice guy. I don't know why you wouldn't."

I cringed. "Not the *nice-guy* thing again."

"Nice guy as in a good person. Not the trade-marked *nice guy*, who is an asshole. There's a difference," she said.

"I like being a good person. I try to be, anyway." Even though I hadn't always been, and my mistake had ruined lives. But I wasn't going to bring that up.

"I don't think I'm ready to make more mistakes than I already have."

"And kissing me would be a mistake," I said bluntly.

She bit her lip. "I think ruining our friendship would be a mistake. I like being your friend, Miles."

The thing was, I liked being her friend, too, so I nodded and picked up the box of pasta. "Are we supposed to salt the water?" I asked, and the relief on her face nearly undid me.

Damn it, the more I told myself I didn't want her, that I shouldn't have her, the harder it was. Clearly, there was something between us. No matter what happened, it wouldn't go anywhere. It couldn't. We had just firmly put each other in our places. And we needed to stay there—even if it hurt.

Seven

Nessa

"Have you had time to finish your paper?" Everly asked as she shelved a few of the new releases.

"Yes, but I'm probably going to spend the night when I get home going over it and making sure it's ready to turn in. I swear, I miss so much reading over it only once or twice."

Everly gave me a small smile. "Considering how hard you worked on it, I'm sure you've already proofed it a few times."

I shrugged. "Yes, Natalie read over it, too. But you know me, I need to make sure it makes sense."

"I'm sure it does."

"And, honestly, I'm not too worried about this class because I'm enjoying myself. The other one? Not so much."

"I thought you said that boy was helping you."

I blushed, shaking my head. "I don't think he's a *boy* if he's nearly twenty-two."

"I'm sorry. I'm now in my thirties, and I feel like I'm aging with each passing day. At least, I'm going to keep telling myself I'm in my thirties, even though I may be in my forties now. I don't remember, and I'm not going to try to do the math."

I laughed and shook my head. "If it helps, you don't look a day over eighty-two."

She shoved my arm playfully and rolled her eyes. "You know, I was going to say that you were in the employee of the month running. But, sorry, I can't do it now. You've ruined your chances."

"We don't even have an employee of the month."

"You were going to be the first one. Then you called me old."

I winked. "You called yourself old first."

"True. I might have. Yet having someone else call me old means it's time to start the firing." She laughed as she said it, and I ducked my head.

"I'm sorry."

"Don't be. My kids called me old the other day because I needed their help opening an app. An *app*.

My generation invented them. And now it seems I'm ancient and need to go sit in my rocker."

"You're not an aging spinster, Everly."

"Some days, I feel like it. But back to what I was asking before. Is that hunky man of yours going to help you with statistics?" Sadly, she didn't fall for my trick of trying to change the subject.

"He's not my man."

"And yet, he *is* hunky," she said, waggling her brows. "And if he's a man and not some eighteen-year-old, that means I can say that."

"Yes, he's a man."

"From the way you said that, it sounds like you want him to be *your* man."

I shook my head as I opened another box of books. "I don't want him to be mine. He's my friend and lives with Pacey and the others. I'm not entertaining another crush on one of the guys who lives in that house."

Everly knew all about my crush on Pacey and my new one on Miles that I wouldn't do anything about. While she was nowhere near old enough to be my mother, I had latched onto Everly when I lost my mom. Just enough that I didn't feel so alone. I had people in my life who cared about me. Including my father. I needed to remember that.

I pushed those thoughts from my mind and tried to

remember what we had been talking about. "As for Miles, yes, he's going to help me with my stats class. We're studying tomorrow to go over my homework. I'm having trouble with a few things, and it probably doesn't help that my mind goes in a thousand different directions sometimes."

"You have a job, a full course load, friends, and maybe, sometimes dating. It's college. Of course, you're tired. And you're working on your final year. It's a lot."

I shrugged. "And now I'm supposed to look at grad schools. But I don't think that's going to happen." I hadn't meant to say that last part aloud.

"No? I thought that was the plan. What's going on, Nessa?"

"It's not a big deal."

"It is. You're talking about getting your master's. And being a professor. And writing your book."

"That's everything I've wanted to do since I was a little kid. And yet, it doesn't seem feasible. It's not going to pay my bills."

"People with English degrees *do* make money. They find careers."

"I'm floundering a bit, and I hate it."

"You've had a few shocks to your system over the past couple of years. It's all right to not have your life together at twenty. I sure didn't. Sometimes, I feel like I never have my life together."

"You have wonderful kids, a growly and glowing husband. I'm pretty sure you do."

Everly smiled even as she shook her head. "And I have bills, sleepless nights… And, hey, my bookstore burned down. Things get complicated."

That made me wince. "I know. It still makes me sad thinking about this place when it burned down."

Everly shuddered. "Me, too. I don't want to think about it. So, we won't. However, I had people to rely on back then, even though I almost didn't see it in time. You have people, too. Including this man-boy," she said with a laugh. "One who is simply your friend but can help with your classes. Are you helping him with anything?"

"Cooking? I don't know. That seems like something he and Natalie do together. Not that I'm jealous. I swear I'm not."

"It didn't sound that way. I swear. It seemed like you knew where the boundaries were and were trying to find a way to repay him."

"Yes, or maybe I'm just tired."

"You're allowed to be. Now, you have thirty minutes left on your shift. Let's go figure out which books you're adding to your pile, and then we can finish setting up the final display."

"I don't know what I'd do for books if I didn't work in a bookstore," I said drily. There was always the library, which I adored and used often, but sometimes I loved the luxury of choice.

"You know, that's what I tell myself about owning one. As it is, Storm won't let me buy any more bookshelves for the house."

"That's sacrilege!"

"Not when there's a bookshelf on every wall in my house, and there's physically no room. However, he's thinking about building me a she-shed just for books."

I nearly swooned. "That's romance. True love."

"Don't I know it. Now, let's pick out your books."

We started up to the front as Miley waved us down. "Nessa, these flowers were delivered for you when you were in the back. A customer was here, so I couldn't call you."

"What?" I asked, confused.

Everly leaned forward. "Oh. Maybe it's the man-boy."

"Please stop calling him that. And I thought it was boy-man."

"I don't know. I'm making things up as I go along. So, who're they from?"

I frowned and looked at the yellow roses mixed with daisies. It was an odd arrangement that seemed happy. I looked at the card and stared at the two women. "I've no idea who they would be from."

"No dates?"

I frowned, shook my head. "One sort of recently. But it didn't work out, and we both agreed on it being the end."

"All right. Well, read the card." Everly tilted her head, studying me.

I pulled the little card out of the envelope and sighed.

Thinking of you. I hope you're having a good day. —Dad.

I blinked. "It's from my dad," I said, frowning. "Why would he spend money on flowers?"

"It was a sweet gesture." I could hear the hesitancy in Everly's voice.

"Maybe. Only Dad doesn't need to spend money on flowers."

"Thank him. He's probably having a stressful time, just like you are. Maybe he needed to do something to make you smile."

I leaned forward, sniffing the roses and the daisies. "I guess so. Although, Dad should know that yellow is my least favorite color. Not that I don't love him and these," I said with a laugh. "Of course, it's Dad. Sometimes those details slip his mind."

"That's guys for you." Everly shook her head.

"Not your guy." Miley smiled. "Storm knows all about you."

"He truly does," I agreed.

Everly clasped her hands against her chest and sighed. "Yes, I'm lucky. One day, you'll be lucky, too. Though, I will say you are already lucky because your father is sending you flowers to make you happy. Don't think about the cost. You're allowed to splurge on happy things."

"Yes, let me text him a thank you, and then we'll get back to the display."

Everly waved me off. "No, text him and then take those flowers home. I know you have homework to do."

"I do," I said with a smile. "Seriously, they are cute."

"And happy," Miley agreed.

I sniffed the blooms again and quickly pulled out my phone.

Me: *Thank you, I love you.*

Dad: *I love you too.*

No more words were needed. I shook my head, packed up my things, and carefully got my flowers out to my car. I buckled them in, grateful for the square base, and made my way home. I had to go over my paper, and I wanted to look at the homework I planned to work through with Miles when he got there the next day.

It would be a long night, but I was used to them. It was college, after all.

I also needed to start looking at financial aid for next semester and investigating other financial avenues. I needed to go to grad school for certain parts of my future dreams. And I would need to get loans to help me through it.

I didn't think working at a bookstore near another university would cut it. I had the applications for grad schools all over my desk, ready to be filled out. I just wasn't there yet. Even though everything was online, I still printed out what I could so I could make a to-do list. It was just a little too much, and I wasn't sure what I was supposed to do.

I pulled into the driveway and parked off to the side, grateful that I was home. I got out of the car and nearly ran into a large body. I looked up and froze.

"Xander?"

"Hey. I was just walking by on the way to a friend's and thought I'd say hi."

Something tingled at the back of my neck but I shrugged it off. I didn't know why he was here. Even if it seemed odd, I didn't want to make things weird—even though it felt strange.

"I didn't know you knew where I lived," I said slowly.

He held up his hands. "One of my friends lives across the way there." He pointed at one of the larger homes where I knew some students lived. "I saw you one day. Totally not stalking," he said with an awkward laugh.

"That's...great?" Things hadn't been awkward when neither of us had offered to go on another date after our last one. Now, they sure as hell felt strange.

"It's good to see you, Nessa. You look great."

"Hmm." I didn't like the look in his eyes, but I wasn't sure what to say. "I have homework to do, and I just got off work. It's nice to see you, Xander."

His eyes warmed, and I knew I probably had said the wrong thing. "It is nice to see you, too. I know we didn't get to firm up any plans for our next date, but I figured since I'm here, why not?"

This was definitely awkward now. We were not on the same page, and I had no idea how to get out of this. I'd never let anyone down before. It wasn't like I'd ever been dumped. Things had just fizzled out naturally. Or didn't fizzle at all, like with Pacey.

"Xander..." I began.

His shoulders fell. "It's like that, is it?"

"You're a nice guy."

He sighed. "Nice guy. Nice guy. It's always the *nice*

guy. I may be nice, but I can be bad, too. Or maybe that's not what you want. Do you want the sizzle? We didn't get that good kiss. You can't just dump me without kissing me."

Alarm shot up my spine. "Xander, I can't dump you because we weren't even dating."

"We *were* dating. We went on two dates. Dating. Went. On. Dates. That's what it's called."

"Xander. I'm sorry. I don't want to say it's not you, it's me, but I'm not in a good place for a relationship right now."

Could I put any more cliches out there? I really wanted to go inside, but he wasn't going to let me. At least, not right now.

"I just think that you need to see what you're missing. And then you'll understand." Before I could take a breath, his hands were on my shoulders, and his lips were plastered to mine. He pushed me back against the car. I froze, not knowing what to do. He forced his tongue into my mouth, and I screamed, pushing him back.

"See? That's what you were missing."

I wiped my mouth with the back of my hand and shook. "No. You don't get to do that."

"Excuse me?" he asked. "I was kissing you. To show you what we could have."

My hands shook, and bile filled my mouth. "Stop.

Go away. I'm sorry, but it's not going to work out, Xander. I didn't want you to kiss me. I didn't let you. You don't get to force that."

"So now you're going to call it forced? All I did was kiss you. Good God, we went on a date. We're dating."

"No, we aren't. Go away." My heart raced, and I swallowed hard. He was blocking my way to the door. I didn't know if anybody was home. I didn't know how I could get out of this. My keys were in my hand. Maybe I could hit him with them, but then what? Could I run fast enough?

"Nessa?" Miles' deep voice reached my ears as he came forward.

Relief filled me, even as Xander glared. "We're talking here." Xander smiled, but the look sent shivers down my spine.

Miles raised a brow. "Nessa? Want to come and stand by me?"

"Gladly." I took a step, but Xander reached out and gripped my arm—hard enough to leave bruises. "Let go," I snapped, pulling away from him.

"We're talking. Get lost," Xander snarled at Miles.

Miles came forward. It was then that I realized how big Miles was. He sometimes hunched his shoulders and looked a little geeky, doing his best not to take up space. But out of all the roommates, Miles was the largest. He was wide, full of muscle, and those broad shoulders were good enough to pit against any hockey player.

"You're going to want to let her go right now," Miles growled.

He wasn't wearing his glasses, and I saw the danger in his eyes.

My heart raced. I just wanted this to end. I wanted to get inside.

"Who the fuck do you think you are?" Xander growled.

"I'm Nessa's friend. You really want to let her go, or I'm going to call the cops."

"The cops? What the fuck is wrong with you?"

I reached out and kicked, lifting my knee. Xander went down, cupping his balls. I practically ran to Miles, mainly because he was between the house and me but also because I wanted to be near him. At his side, I wasn't alone.

My heart raced, and I couldn't keep up with my thoughts. So, when Miles took my hand, I freely clung to him and stood slightly behind him. Not entirely, but enough that I felt safer.

I could not believe that I was cowering like this, but I *had* kneed him. I had fought back.

"You're going to want to fucking go, or we *are* going to call the cops," Miles bit out.

"Go, Xander," I blurted, wanting this over.

Xander stumbled up and glared. "Fine," he snapped. "I see there's been a misunderstanding." He held up both hands. "I'll go."

And then he stomped off toward whatever house he had supposedly been going to, and my knees began to shake. "I think I need to go inside."

"I've got you," Miles said, and then he picked up my bag, the one I hadn't even realized I'd dropped, and practically carried me into the house.

The lights were off, and that's when I realized that Natalie's car wasn't in the garage. She wasn't here. I *had* been alone. Truly alone. And then Miles was there.

"I just…how are you here? What the hell just happened? My flowers."

Miles blinked at me, went to the fridge, and pulled out a bottle of vodka. "Is this the only alcohol you have?" he asked.

"That and some terrible wine."

"Do you want a shot?"

"I hate the taste of vodka, but yes."

He gave me a look, a tight nod, and then pulled out a 7Up. He poured a shot of vodka into two glasses, put in some ice, and poured the soda over it before handing me one. He clinked our glasses, and each of us chugged quickly.

The bubbles of the soda tickled my nose. The

vodka burned, but I calmed down, looking at the empty glass in my hand.

I hadn't even realized I had sat down in my kitchen or that Miles had closed the door behind us.

"What were you saying?"

"My flowers. My dad got me an arrangement. It's still in my car."

Miles sighed and held out his hand. "Give me your keys. I'll make sure that it gets inside."

"I should be fine going out there. I'm an adult. Only what if he's out there?"

"Are we going to call the cops?"

I let out a breath. "I'm going to need to. I should have just now, but I didn't. That was probably the wrong decision, but I don't know what I'm supposed to do at all."

"It's fine. You're fine." He knelt in front of me. That's when I realized he was wearing gray sweatpants, running shoes, and a sweatshirt.

"Were you jogging?"

He nodded. "I needed to think, and I do better when I jog or lift weights. Wasn't in the mood to lift tonight."

"That's why you have so many muscles." I was rambling now, but I didn't care.

His cheeks reddened. "Probably. When I get stressed, I work out, do math, or play video games. In other words, I do anything *but* deal with what's stressing me. Much like this conversation."

"I can't believe he did that," I whispered, tears threatening to fall.

Miles remained kneeling in front of me. I hadn't realized he was still holding my hands until I looked down at his large palms against mine.

"What happened?"

"I don't know. Xander said he was walking by, much like you just were," I said softly.

He narrowed his eyes. "You live down the block from me. I always run this way because you have bigger sidewalks than the other street. You've seen me running in front of your house before."

I cringed. "Yes, I'm sorry. I wasn't comparing you."

"I get it. It's fine. Now, I think we're going to call the cops, we're going to call the girls, and then we're going to figure out what to do."

I froze. "The girls?"

"We need to tell them and maybe the guys so they can be on the lookout. We're your friends, Nessa. Let us take care of you."

I nodded, knowing he was right. "Tomorrow. We'll call the cops now, but we'll tell the girls tomorrow. They're all doing their own things, and I don't want to ruin their nights."

"Nessa."

"Please? I always feel like I'm the one people have to come and rescue."

"You know that is the farthest thing from the truth," he growled.

"Can I just have tonight?"

He sighed.

"I'll tell the girls tomorrow, I promise," I said.

"Okay. Then I'm spending the night," he stated, and I widened my eyes.

"What?"

"If the girls aren't here, I'm sleeping on your couch. It's either that or we bundle you up and you stay at our house. But then you'd have to tell them what happened. I get that you're going to need a moment to think, and that's fine. But I'm staying the night. You're not going to be alone."

"Okay," I whispered.

He studied my face and gave me a tight nod. "Okay, then. I'm going to go save your plant."

That made me laugh. "I think they're just flowers, not a plant."

He snorted. "I'll save your flowers, then. And *then* we're going to call the cops. After that, I'm going to get to know your couch. You have school in the morning, and then you're going to tell the girls everything. Got me?"

"I didn't know you were so bossy." My face felt a

little warm, hopefully just from the vodka.

"You don't know a lot of things about me, Nessa. But it seems you're about to learn some." He walked off, and I did my best not to look at him go or notice how those gray sweatpants fit him.

My head ached, and I reached for my phone, knowing I would have to go over everything more than once. I wasn't ready. Miles would be back soon, and he'd help. And, somehow, I'd do my best not to lean on him.

Somehow.

.

EIGHT

Miles

I paced the kitchen and tried to catch my breath, passing the others as they each grumbled to one another.

"You called the cops?" Tanner asked.

I rolled on him. "What else was I supposed to do?"

Tanner held up both hands. "I'm just making sure you did, not saying that you made a mistake in doing so. Jesus Christ. She okay?"

I shook my head and slid my hand through my hair. "I think so. She says she is. Fuck, she could have been badly hurt."

"I'm just glad you were there," Tanner said, his hands fisted in front of him on the counter.

Pacey let out a breath. "I don't know what I would've done if she had been hurt any more than she already was."

I looked at Pacey and tried not to let any of my resentment show. I knew my roommate hadn't meant to string Nessa along. The situation had been an accident since Pacey hadn't seen the longing etched on Nessa's face. Yet Pacey had hurt Nessa, even if he hadn't meant to. I knew the two were on better terms now, but I couldn't help but be a little jealous of what she had felt for the guy.

Only that was on me and had nothing to do with the fact that this asshole, Xander, had hurt Nessa.

Dillon turned to me. "Do you know what the police are doing?"

"They took her statement and mine, and I know they were going to go talk to the guy, but I don't know anything beyond that."

"It's not like you had any evidence," Tanner grumbled. "I don't think they can go and arrest him. It sounds to me like they'll warn him or ask him some questions."

Dillon growled. "Xander is just like Sanders. Slick. He's probably able to get away with anything."

"As much as I hate Sanders, I don't see him doing what Xander did," Pacey growled.

I nodded tightly. "True, but Xander is that slick kind of guy."

Dillon cleared his throat. "If I remember right, his dad's a big-time lawyer."

I looked at Dillon. "You know Xander?"

"Not beyond a couple of classes. I vaguely remember him saying something along those lines, though."

"Crap," I growled.

"We'll do what we can. Nessa is safe at the house. The doors are locked," Pacey added.

Tanner nodded. "Yes, I changed them, mainly because the door was about to fall off anyway. The landlord didn't mind. Though, of course, they didn't. I was doing the work for them for free."

"Is there anything else we can do to keep them safe?" I asked, worry gnawing at my gut.

"Unless they let us put in a security system I can't afford, I'm not sure," Tanner said.

"If it's the money, I can handle that," Pacey growled. "Our house has better security, but it's not like we can move all four girls in here." Pacey paused. "Well, we could, but then our girlfriends would be living with us, and that might be a little weird."

I narrowed my eyes. "And what about the other girls?"

"If all else fails, they can share Sanders' old room."

Nessa could stay in mine, but I didn't say that. Nor would I even think that again. Because that was wrong. So wrong.

"The point is moot," I said, shaking my head. "The girls aren't going to want to live here, and that's not the point anyway."

"No, the point is we need to do whatever we can to make sure they feel safe."

"Sometimes, I don't know how the hell we make it through these things," Dillon grumbled before he drank the last of his coffee.

"I don't know, either." Pacey looked blankly at the kitchen window, his shoulders drooping.

I looked over at Tanner. "Thank you for taking care of the locks."

"I'm just glad I did it. I don't want to think…no, I'm not going to think about what might have happened if I hadn't," Tanner grumbled.

"If the authorities don't, we'll do what we can to make sure Xander stays away from her," Pacey said, nodding tightly.

"I'm going over there to help with her stats homework. I'll talk to her."

Pacey gave me a look, and I shrugged. "We're friends." Just because I wanted more didn't mean anything.

"None of the girls are alone. Ever," Pacey said.

Tanner barked out a laugh, and I glared at him.

"What?" I asked.

"Yes, because us doing our best to rally around them and force them never to be alone and always be taken care of will go over *so* well with these women. Two of you are dating them. You should know better than that."

Pacey shrugged. "I'll still do what I can to protect them."

I sighed. "We all will. Now, I need to head over."

"I'm sure all of us will go at some point to check on them," Dillon said with a shrug. "It's what we do."

I nodded. "I know. I wish I could've been the one to hit him." I shook my head. "You should've seen Nessa. She was magnificent." The guys gave me a look, and I knew I had probably said too much.

I nodded and then headed out, grabbing my books. I was decent at statistics and had taken the same class that she was in, so I should be of some help. Honestly, I just wanted to spend time with her—even if that was probably a mistake.

I walked the distance to their house so I didn't have to park on the street, and it helped me burn off some of my energy. I was too wired when it came to Nessa, especially with what had happened in her driveway. It was all just a little too much, and I hated that I hadn't been able to do anything but growl and do my best to protect her. She'd defended herself, and I had slept on their damn couch. The lumpy thing had given me a crick in the neck, but when Natalie had come home the next morning after spending the night at her parents' house, her eyes had gone wide. I had left before Nessa could explain to everyone what had happened.

Still, I had been there. Sleeping under the same roof as Nessa. Even though she had slept in my bed before, I hadn't been there with her. She'd been drunk, had kissed me, and I'd walked away, leaving her in my room. An event she didn't remember, and one I told myself to forget.

I knocked on the door. Nessa opened it after a moment, looking through the chain. "Hey," she said quickly before closing the door again, undoing the chain, and opening the door for me.

"Hey there," I said, feeling awkward.

"I'd ask how you are, but you're the one who had to sleep on that couch. I can guess."

I shrugged as I set my bag down on the coffee table. "I didn't mind. I just didn't want you to be alone."

Nessa looked at me and bit her lip. "I'm glad you were here. Even though I kind of resented it at the time."

My eyebrows winged up. "Why would you resent it?"

"I hated that I couldn't do it all on my own. And I don't like becoming a statistic. The cops said they would talk to him. But, apparently, his dad is a lawyer and already on it."

"That's what we figured," I grumbled.

She narrowed her eyes. "We?"

I sat down on the couch and rolled my neck. "The guys. Of course, we talked about it, Nessa. I'm honestly surprised they didn't come here with me, stomping and following me around."

She snorted. "They'll probably be here in like thirty minutes."

I shook my head. "No, they know I'm here."

"Ah, so you guys are going to rotate?"

"Maybe. I'll have you know it's better than the alternative."

She narrowed her eyes and then sighed. "They want us to all move in there, don't they?"

"Yes. You and Natalie could share Sanders' old room."

"Oh, that's nice. We lose our house and are safe with the big, bad men who will protect us from everything. And, suddenly, the guys are living with their girlfriends. That's a big step. But, sure, the sad little single girls can share the smallest room in the house."

"I think Tanner's room is the smallest."

She laughed. "Great, that's so helpful."

"Just making conversation."

"I hate this conversation."

"That guy attacked you," I said. "I fucking hated *that.*"

"I don't know what we're supposed to do. How am I supposed to pretend like it didn't happen? But I'm going to try. I have work, school, and my life."

"Did you tell your dad?" I asked softly.

She shook her head, and I cursed. "Don't curse at me. I don't know how to tell him that I was attacked. We reported it. The girls know. The guys know. Dad doesn't need to know right now. He has enough on his plate."

Something in her tone worried me. "What do you mean by that?"

She shook her head. "I don't want to talk about it."

I searched her face before nodding, then pulled out my textbook. "Let's get through some statistics, and then maybe you can show me how to cook something," I said, trying to relieve the tension.

She smiled up at me. "I can do that."

I sat next to her on the couch and felt her heat. I couldn't help but wonder what the hell I was doing. I should stay away from her. Yes, I wanted to protect her. Yes, I wanted her to be okay. But being next to her?

Being next to the girl I'd had a crush on for over a year now, the one I kept thinking about, even though she wasn't for me? That was masochistic.

I couldn't hold back. Yet, I couldn't stay away.

"Why are you looking at me like that?" she whispered.

I swallowed hard. "What?"

"He didn't hurt me, Miles. Not really. I'm fine." She rubbed her arm.

I narrowed my eyes. "Did he hurt you for real?"

"No. No bruises. I thought he might leave one on my arm, but nothing formed."

"I wish I could just punch him and make things better, but I know violence doesn't solve things."

"I don't know, kneeing him in the balls was kind of nice."

I snorted. "Kind of sad I wasn't the one to do that."

"I'm just glad I could take care of myself."

"You could. You did. It was pretty damn amazing."

"Thanks," she whispered, and her gaze went to my mouth. At least, I thought it did.

"There's something you should know," she said after a moment.

I looked down at her. "What?" I asked, my voice soft, barely above a whisper.

"I remember."

I blinked and looked at her. "What do you remember?"

"I remember the kiss. I remember acting like an idiot and drinking too much. I remember how sweet you were, how you took care of me. But I remember the kiss, Miles. And I want to apologize."

My heart raced, and I tried to keep up. She remembered? After all this time, she remembered. And she hadn't said a thing.

I shook my head. "You remember us kissing."

"I remember me kissing you and practically forcing myself on you." She shuddered.

I reached out and gripped her hand. She looked down at it, and I swallowed hard. "You didn't force me to kiss you. I didn't kiss you. You were drunk, and I wasn't about to do anything to hurt you. I remember, too. I wanted to kiss you. Damn it, Nessa, I've wanted to kiss you for a long time. So don't fucking apologize."

Her eyes widened, and I hated that I had probably said too much.

"You wanted to kiss me? For a long time? I don't understand."

"Forget I said anything. Let's worry about school and classes and all of that. I shouldn't have said anything."

"No, you should. You should talk to me. I thought

you didn't want to talk about it because you regretted it."

"Hell, no. I didn't regret it. I don't. Other than the fact that you were hurting and drunk, and I was trying to put you to bed when you kissed me. I thought you didn't remember it, and I didn't want to bring it up because that would have been awkward as fuck. Probably as awkward as it is right now."

She stood up and began to pace. I stood, as well, not wanting to sit when she was standing.

"You *wanted* to kiss me."

"Nessa, every time I'm near you, I want to kiss you. Only you never wanted me. We both know who you wanted."

She looked at me then, and I stuffed my hands into my pockets. If I didn't, I knew I would want to reach out and touch her. And I shouldn't. I knew damn well that I shouldn't.

"I don't want Pacey. Not anymore. It was just a crush that got twisted in my head. I kept making a fool of myself because of it. Pacey's still my friend and he always will be, but I didn't love him like I thought I did. And that's on me. I kissed you. Maybe because I was drinking and thinking about you and anything but what I *should* have been thinking of. But I only regret that I was stupid about it. I didn't hate it, Miles. And the problem is, I keep thinking about you, too. And I shouldn't."

"You keep thinking about me, too," I repeated.

"Of course, I do. You're sweet, and you're nice, and…stop looking at me like that," Nessa warned. I shrugged.

"There's that *nice* thing again."

"No, you are a *good* guy. Not just a nice guy. Xander was the *nice guy*, who ended up being a douche. You are not that guy."

I narrowed my eyes. "I don't appreciate you comparing me to him."

"I'm sorry. I won't."

"It's fine," I whispered.

"Yes, I had a crush on Pacey, thinking that I wanted more. The reality is, we are much better as friends. And I see how he is with Mackenzie. They're just perfect, you know? They're fated and all of that. Like one of the romances I love to read."

"They are pretty amazing together," I whispered.

"He was never for me. It took me a long time to realize that and get my head out of my ass. Yes, I had a crush on Pacey. But that's over. It's just that every time I look at you, I remember that kiss and how much I liked it, even though I shouldn't remember it. I'm done hiding the fact that I did."

"You liked it."

"You keep repeating everything that I say."

I laughed then. "Of course, I am. I have no idea what's going on," I whispered.

"I don't know, either," she whispered back.

"Okay, then. So, we both remember and liked the kiss. I keep thinking about you, and you keep thinking about me." I had no idea if I was still dreaming or if I'd suddenly woken up in a new reality, but this didn't feel real. It *couldn't* be real.

"There's so much going on in my life, Miles. I don't want to risk our friendship for something that will probably blow up in our faces."

I took a step forward and swallowed hard. "I get it." I paused. "Still…"

She reached out and put her hand on my chest. I reached for her, as well, running my fingers down her arm. "Still," she echoed, then she went onto her tiptoes and brushed her lips across mine.

I was so much taller than her that I had to hunch slightly so she could press her lips to mine. I kissed her softly, needing her taste but going slow. After all, the incident with Xander had only been the night before, and we had just been talking about Pacey. There were so many reasons not to do this, but I couldn't stop. I didn't want to.

I kissed her again and then pulled away, my breath coming in pants even though it had been a gentle kiss.

"I've been thinking about that for a long time," I whispered.

"Me, too. But, Miles, we only have a year left of school, and then we're all moving away. Things are changing, and there's so much going on in our lives. I can't do a relationship. I thought I could at least pretend to date somebody to get over Pacey, but that wasn't the case. I'm already over him."

I nodded. "I know. At the end of the year, we both move away. We'll always be friends, but things will change." I didn't know why that hurt so much to say, but I had to put it out there.

"I like kissing you," she said softly, and I smiled.

"I like kissing you, too." I leaned down and kissed her again. "Just for this year. Or for however long it lasts. Because I can't stop thinking about you, Nessa. And I'm tired of pretending."

She looked up at me then. "Friendship first. Always. Even if this is a mistake."

"Friendship first. Always." Then I leaned down and kissed her again, wondering when exactly I would wake up from this dream.

NINE

Nessa

I let out a breath and closed my computer. I was still waiting on news about a few grants and for some letters of recommendation. It was as if I had to pretend that I was still going through with my grad school plans, even if I felt like I was behind. However, none of that was what I was working on at the moment.

While I bit my lip and tapped my foot, I waited on emails from my agent. I hadn't told anybody that I had written a trilogy. An actual trilogy that I was excited about. I knew that if I got the first book picked up as it was being shopped, the second and third would probably have to be entirely reworked—if not discarded. But the books had poured out of me, and I had taken nearly my entire college career to get them to the point where I was ready. Somehow, through my persistence and sheer luck, I'd landed an agent. And now, we were shopping my work.

I'd known I wanted to be a writer from a young age. My mother had dreamed that I would write a book, and I had finished the first one right before she passed. She had been my first beta reader and probably my harshest critic. Tough love because she had wanted me to succeed, even when she said she loved it.

I just hoped the rest of the world embraced it. It was my dream, even though I knew that I would have to get a big-girl job and not just work at a bookstore. What English professor wasn't working on a book in their spare time? It was a given. First, though, I needed to get into grad school and possibly even work on my doctorates before starting anything else.

Only, now, I didn't even know if I would be able to finish this semester. I sighed and nearly jolted out of my chair at my small desk in my bedroom when someone knocked on the door.

Elise spoke through the door. "Nessa? There are flowers for you. Are they from Miles? I know you have a date tonight."

I got out of my chair and rolled my shoulders back, stretching since I had been sitting too long. A nervous smile played on my face as I thought over her words. I *did* have a date with Miles tonight. An actual date, though one where we knew there was no future because we were both moving on with whatever lives we picked and were chosen for after this year. I still couldn't believe I had kissed him or that he had kissed me. I would probably make another mistake at some point, but at least I would go into it face-forward. It was relaxing to be around Miles, even though parts of me were *never* relaxed around him.

I opened the door and frowned. "Flowers?" I asked as I looked at the bouquet of yellow wildflowers in Elise's hands.

"There's no note, but I assume they're from Miles."

I shook my head. "I don't think so. Don't you think he would have them in his hand when he shows up in a little bit?" I asked, confused and a little worried. I didn't know why, but something felt off.

Elise scrunched her nose. "You don't think they're from..." Her voice trailed off, and her eyes widened.

"No. I mean, they couldn't be. Xander wouldn't send me flowers." Those yellow flowers from the bookshop filled my mind, but my dad had signed the card for those. These didn't have a note. It was really weird.

"I don't know. I'll ask Miles. Or, I don't know. What should I do?"

"Maybe we should call that detective," Elise offered.

"I'm not sure. It seems like I'd be blowing things out of proportion if I do."

"Who are we calling?" Mackenzie came toward us and stood, hands on her hips. "You got flowers?"

"Apparently. I just don't know who they're from."

"Let's just put them down." Elise set the bouquet on the table in the hallway. "Maybe we should take a picture. I don't know. Why am I so paranoid?"

"We're all paranoid," I added as I rubbed my hands on my jeans. "It's just weird. But there's not anything we can do about it, is there?"

Mackenzie let out a breath. "No. But maybe we should call and check it just in case. Report it."

I frowned. "And say that we got random flowers and don't know who they're from?"

Mackenzie leaned forward. "Maybe they can check who sent them. Do we know the name of the driver?"

Elise shook her head. "No, they just showed up at the house. I checked through the peephole. They said they had a delivery for Nessa, and then I told them to leave them on the porch. I didn't even open the door until they were gone." Elise groaned into her hands. "I was trying to be smart about it."

"That *was* smart. We'll figure it out. I'll probably still report it because there has to be something here. If it's not Xander, then… I'm just paranoid."

"Go get ready for your date," Mackenzie said as she nodded tightly. "We'll handle this."

I sucked in a breath. "You guys, they were addressed to me."

Elise nodded. "We'll handle that, too. However, you need to get ready. We love you."

"We're here for you. No matter what." Mackenzie turned me around and slapped me on the ass before pushing me into my room.

"Did you just slap me?" I asked, laughing.

"You know, guys do it in sports. Why can't I do it here?"

"I don't know if that's what you should base your spanking on." Elise snorted. "Anyway, we'll handle this. You get ready."

"We're only going to a little diner," I said before I took a deep breath. "Not the same one Xander took me to."

Mackenzie nodded. "Good. No need to double that trouble."

"So, I'm just going to dinner. No need to dress up, right? It's only Miles. It's not like I'm going on a real date with him. This is ridiculous. We're friends, and we both said we didn't want to ruin our relationship. And, hell, I make abysmal decisions when it comes to guys—no offense, Mackenzie."

Mackenzie held up both hands. "No offense taken. Remember who my ex is?"

"She's got you there," Elise said, and Mackenzie rolled her eyes.

"Seriously, though, just have fun. You both said you're looking to have that. It doesn't even have to be about sex," Mackenzie added.

My eyes widened. "I'm not having sex tonight, am I?" I asked.

Elise raised a brow. "No, you're not having sex tonight. Not if you don't want to."

"Not that I *don't* want to because…have you seen Miles?"

"Oh, we have," Mackenzie added with a wink.

I rolled my eyes. "I'm not ready to have sex. I don't even know if I'm ready to date."

"Why?" Elise asked.

We turned as Natalie came into the hallway, as well. "Yes, tell us why you are so afraid to go on a date with the lovely and sweet Miles."

My heart twisted. "What if I hurt him? What if this isn't a crush? Why the hell do I keep having crushes on the roommates? Again, no offense, Mackenzie."

"You have remarkable taste," Mackenzie said, her voice soft.

"The thing is, I thought I had feelings for Pacey that were more than they were, and it twisted me up inside. It almost hurt you and Pacey in the process. I realize that we are so much better now, but I don't want to be that person again. Only, here I am, about to go on a date with another of the guys."

Natalie sighed. "Those four men are great. Except for Tanner, but you're not going on a date with Tanner."

I snorted. "No, that won't be happening. But Tanner's a good guy, too."

"Yes, and he's handy around the house. But he's sometimes a judge-y asshole. However, I digress." Natalie sighed, shaking her head. "You are going out on a nice date with a sweet guy, and what are you going to do? You're going to have coffee with him. Or dinner at the diner or whatever. You're going to enjoy yourself. Get to know him beyond him being your study friend. And then maybe kiss him because I know you've done that before. Then, you'll come home, do more work on your book or homework, and then go to bed. Not everything we do in college when it comes to those we date has to be forever. Elise and Mackenzie may have found theirs, and I say *may* because, hello, we're still in college. And I'm not going to go crazy and say marriage. We're allowed to date and have fun and not think about big, grandiose plans."

The three of us just stared at Natalie and her big speech. The woman blushed.

"What? I may be a virgin, but it's not because I'm saving myself for marriage. I just have to like the guy I'm going to sleep with. I tend to not like a lot of the guys around me because I'm awkward and I talk too quickly, and then they think I'm too stuck up or too much of a virgin, so they don't want to touch this unless they want me to be another notch on their bedpost. It's not my fault that everybody keeps snatching up all the good guys. Again, all your fault. But I love you." She laughed, and I shook my head.

"I don't want forever," I said. "I don't even know what I want beyond this moment, but I said I was going on a date, and I will. Those flowers..." I let my voice trail off.

"We will deal with the flowers," Mackenzie said, nodding tightly. "Natalie, go get her dressed and ready to go on her date. We will handle this. When we need you, we will get you. You're going to have fun tonight, damn it. Miles is a great guy. Have fun, kiss a bit, and then just come home. You do not have to do anything you don't want to do. We love you." Elise leaned forward and kissed me on the cheek. Mackenzie did the same.

Natalie practically skipped into the room and closed the door behind her. "Okay. First, what flowers?" She laughed. "Let's get you ready."

I swallowed hard and stared at my friend. I knew I needed to do this.

There was so much going on inside me. I could barely think. I was usually the one prone to fun and going with the flow—like Corinne—but that had led me down the wrong paths. I wasn't a planner as much as the others were, but I needed to be. And right now, I would be. Finally.

I sat across the table from Miles, feeling slightly awkward yet not knowing what to say.

"I would ask how your burger is, but I think I already did that," Miles said as he played with a fry. I winced and looked up at him. "Why are we so bad at this?" I asked, my eyes widening. "Not that you're bad. I'm the bad one. I should know how to speak to you. We talk all the time."

"We do," he said, his voice soft. "I think both of us spent so long not talking about that kiss that it gave us something to ramble about. In other words, everything else."

I cringed. "I'm not good at this. As evidenced by my very scattered dating history."

Miles snorted. "Pretty sure mine is worse than yours. I've never had a serious relationship."

"Me, either. I had a lasting crush, and we know how that ended up." I cringed. "I shouldn't bring up Pacey when we're on a date."

"He's my roommate, your best friend. He's going to come up. You guys handled that, haven't you?" I could hear the hesitancy in his voice.

"Yes, we took care of it, even though I'm still sometimes like an awkward little turtle in front of him."

He started. "I haven't heard that phrase in a while."

"My mom says it, and then I say it, too. It just happens." I paused, my eyes widening. "I meant my mom *said* it. Wow, sometimes I don't even realize that I go present tense on her. I feel like she's still here, you know? Maybe I shouldn't bring up my mother right now."

"You should. We should talk about those we've lost." Something in his tone told me I shouldn't touch on exactly what he meant by that, so I didn't. But I did want to know. His expression closed off just slightly, so while he wanted me to talk about my mother, he wasn't ready to talk about someone. I understood. Things hurt.

"My mom passed away pretty quickly. The cancer seemingly came out of nowhere and hit her hard. We tried every treatment we could, but in the end, nothing we did worked. I think we're doing okay now, although the bills keep coming, and it gets a little insane. Plus, I have no idea how I'm going to pay for this semester. But, here we are." I groaned and put my hands on my face. "Why am I like this? You didn't need to know that."

Miles reached across the table. "What are you talking about, Nessa? I knew about your mom. You've talked about it before. But bills? You're not going to finish school?"

I looked up at him. "I'm trying to get a scholarship because I don't qualify for the rest of the loans I need for the last semester. I have so much debt as it is, and I don't want to go the rest of my life with student loan debt piled on top of me until I'm eighty. I'm thinking about using the rest of my college fund I have saved to help my dad pay for bills, because even though he says he can keep the house, I just don't know. So, here I am, thinking about dropping out of college, right at the last bit, and maybe finishing up at a community college. I don't know. Maybe working somewhere that will let you come in with only a semi-English degree. I don't have a plan, and I'm freaking out. The bookstore pays well—as well as it can—and I get benefits through my dad's work while I'm still in school, so that makes it even more difficult. I have no idea what I'm talking about. I should go."

My heart raced, and I honestly couldn't believe I'd said all of that in one big rush. I hadn't meant to say *any* of it, but now I couldn't take the words back and pretend I hadn't said them.

Miles squeezed my hand, and I looked up at him. And then he got out of the booth and came to sit down next to me. Nobody was paying attention to us, but I still blushed. "What are you doing?"

"We're going to ask for the check, and then we're going back to my place to watch a movie and relax. You're my friend, Nessa. And it's clear you're going through a hell of a lot. I'll figure out a way to help you. I have a feeling you haven't talked about money problems with the rest of the girls or Pacey or anyone."

"It's embarrassing."

"It's only that way because we're told we have to be embarrassed about money. The fact that you're thinking about dropping out of school to help your dad is noble. But there are things we can do. You have a semester and a half left. I know you can get a refund for the semester if you drop out now, but let's just think about it as one semester left. You're so close. We can help."

"Miles, it's more difficult than that."

"Maybe. Or perhaps if we put eight heads together, we can figure it all out. I know Tanner is on a few different scholarships. Same as Dillon. I'm on academic ones for my major, so I'm no help there. But I can find something. Plus, you want to go to grad school. It's your plan and something you sort of need for the career you want. It sucks, but I'm the same way. I'm looking at programs that pay for me. Meaning, I have to move to a completely different state at this point. I get it. We *can* make this happen, though."

"Miles," I said, my chest warming at the way he wanted to help me and take care of everything. Yes, I could try to do everything myself, but I wasn't doing well at that, was I? Maybe I needed help. He kissed the top of my head, and I blushed. "Come on. We'll get the check, take our cold burgers home because I'm not about to waste food, and we'll watch a movie."

"They probably won't be good warmed up."

"I can eat cold burgers. We're college students. We're supposed to live on this and ramen." I sighed, and when he got the check, I swallowed hard and tried to tell myself that this was just friends hanging out. I liked him. He was sweet and tried his best to take care of everybody, even though I wasn't sure who took care of *him*. Maybe that could be me. At least, for as long as we had each other. I didn't need to put the entire world on my shoulders right in this instant.

We gathered our food and paid, each of us taking half the bill since I knew he was worried about money, too. And then he tangled his fingers with mine as we walked back to the car. It was a short drive, and we talked about nothing important on the way, just classes.

I could hear voices in the kitchen when we got to Miles' place, but we kept going all the way upstairs.

"I have a mini-fridge up here with sodas and water so we don't have to go and talk to anybody if you don't want to."

"I know I need to tell everybody everything," I said, the flowers coming to mind. Nothing had come of that yet, and I should tell him. And I would. Only not now. I'd had enough drama for one night, and I just wanted to breathe.

He pulled me to the couch in the corner, and I looked around the room. "Your room's huge."

"It's not that big. Dillon's and Pacey's are bigger. And if you make a dick joke about that, I am walking out of here right now," he warned as I laughed.

"Stop making me laugh. My side hurts."

He growled before shaking his head. "I have no one to blame but myself."

"Pretty much." I sat next to him on the couch, looked up at him, and everything else just flew out of my mind. Yes, there were money and future problems. But right now, my friend was holding me. Miles was here with those very kissable lips. And there was only one thing I could do. I kissed him. Miles froze for a moment, and I was afraid I had moved too fast. But then he leaned into me, kissed me again, and I groaned. He nipped at my lip, and I slid my hand over his cheek. His hand moved to my hip, and I could barely breathe. I pulled away. My chest heaved, and his glasses had fogged up slightly. It was so damn hot.

"Miles?"

"Nessa?" he asked, his voice low, a growl so full of need that I wanted to jump him right then. I couldn't.

"Miles, I'm not sleeping with you," I blurted, suddenly needing to find a rock to hide under.

Quickly.

Ten

Miles

I blinked at Nessa's words. "Okay."

"I'm sorry. I mean maybe later, but not right now."

I did my best to push images of sex with Nessa out of my mind, but given that she had just said "sex" while practically on top of me, and I could feel her heat, and my cock was hard, it was a little difficult to focus.

"Anything you want. I wasn't expecting—damn it." I let out a breath and did my best to keep images of what Nessa had said out of my mind. "I didn't expect anything tonight. I promise. I'm sorry. If that's what you thought... I'm so sorry."

She winced. "That's not what I meant. I was only trying to put it out there that I didn't want to sleep with you tonight. I didn't mean that I didn't want to sleep with you ever. I don't want to mess with our friendship, so I want to take it slow. I hope that makes sense."

I nodded quickly, relief and disappointment warring inside of me. "Of course. Same here."

"I guess that means we're taking things slow. I'm not ready for sex. It complicates everything. And my life is super involved as it is. I have a feeling if we have sex, it'll only make things harder." She blushed, and I did my best not to laugh. "You know what I mean."

"My mind went somewhere else, but yes, I understand what you mean." My dick did indeed get hard, but I ignored it.

"I don't want you to think I'm leading you on or being a tease or anything."

I frowned and shook my head. "Of course, not. I don't think you're a tease, Nessa. I think we should take it slow, too. And unlike some people I know, I don't have sex on the first date. Sometimes not even the second. I'm not a guy who just bangs and walks away. Which probably isn't the best thing to say when you're nearly on my lap." She looked down, and her eyes widened. I resisted the urge to cover myself.

"Oh. I didn't think. Um, that's good to know. However, I would like to watch that movie. And maybe kiss. I like kissing."

My gaze shot to her lips. "I like kissing, too."

"I'm not using you, Miles. Not to get over anyone or to forget about life. You're my friend, okay?"

That made me smile, and I reached out, brushing the hair from her face to tuck it behind her ear. "I'm the same. I'm not using you, either. If we end up using each other just a little, then we do it beneficially, where we know what we want going in. Together." I frowned.

She leaned into my touch, and I swallowed hard. It was so hard to think when she was touching me, but I did my best.

"Yes. Exactly." When she leaned forward, I met her halfway and brushed my lips across hers. She tasted of coffee and Nessa. I held back a groan, knowing that kissing her would soon become an addiction. I'd been thinking about it since I first met her, and that had been over a year ago. She hadn't been for me then—at least that's what I had told myself.

Were things different now? I wasn't sure. But maybe I wanted them to be. I kissed her, deepening it slightly until we both moaned. Slowly, I brushed my lips across hers and then along her jaw as she tilted her head, giving me better access. She groaned, the soft sound going straight to my cock, and I knew I'd end up with zipper marks later. I didn't care. She was so soft, so sweet. So precious. I didn't want to break her, and I was a big guy. So, I would have to be gentle—oh, so gentle.

I slowly slid my hands down her sides and over her hips. I squeezed, and she moved, pressing her body against my side. When we each sucked in a breath, she repositioned herself to straddle me, her heat right above my dick. I told myself I would stop thinking about her pussy. Only I couldn't. Not even a little. She was so close, only her jeans and mine separating us. It was all I could do not to rise and rub against her. I couldn't stop thinking about her pussy, and her breasts, and everything about her. Damn it. I liked Nessa. I wouldn't let my mind wander more than it already had. I would kiss her and nothing else. And then I groaned. Loudly. She froze for a moment before grinning at me and leaning down to bite my lip as she slowly rocked against me.

I sucked in a breath through my teeth and counted to ten. I would not come in my jeans like a fucking teenager. I'd had sex before. I could last, damn it. I would not come. No, no, no. No coming.

I put one hand on her hip, keeping her steady because the friction was getting to me, and then I slid the other into her hair. I tugged slightly, testing, and her pupils widened as she gasped.

"You like?" I asked tentatively. I liked things a little rougher despite what some may think about me, but I would be gentle with her. I would be anything Nessa wanted and needed me to be.

"I do," she said. Once again, I nearly came.

I tugged again, this time a little harder, and her mouth parted in a sigh. Since her head was already dropped back, I pressed a kiss to her throat before nibbling down to her shoulder, licking and biting along the way. She groaned, rocking her hips again. I tugged on her hair harder because I knew she liked it—I saw it in her face, heard it in how she moaned.

I'd give her what she wanted and take what I needed. It would all be mutually beneficial because that's what I got off on. I liked it hard and rough, but I knew I'd like it however she wanted.

The fact that she liked me tugging on her hair a bit? Fucking perfect.

Testing, I took one of her wrists and pulled it behind her back. It brought her breasts closer to my face, and I rubbed my cheek against one of the soft mounds over her shirt. She groaned, pushing closer to my face, and since they were right there, I nuzzled both, biting through the fabric a bit. She moaned louder, and I used my hand, already holding one wrist, to grasp the other. I pinned her arms behind her, bringing her chest even closer. She looked at me.

"Good?" I asked, needing consent.

"Yes," she said, her breath getting choppy. I kept both arms pinned behind her with one hand as I slowly rubbed my other finger along her collarbone and down into the deep V of her shirt. She had a tank on underneath, so I slowly brushed my finger across the swell of her breasts under her tank. Her mouth parted, and she began breathing in soft pants, squeezing her thighs against my hips. I kept my gaze on her as I slowly tugged her shirt down, taking her tank and her bra with it. She blinked at me before leaning down to kiss me. I kissed her harder than before, not bruising but with a little more need. She groaned again. I tugged her shirt down farther, pinning her arms in place a bit more as I slowly revealed her breasts. "Miles," she panted more.

"Just tell me when to stop."

"I can't," she whispered. "I won't."

I slowly brushed my knuckle across her nipple, watching it pebble into a hard point against my skin. I leaned down, breathed cool air over it, and it puckered beautifully. She was so pink, so beautiful. I leaned down and sucked a taut bud into my mouth, a little harder than I might have meant. She moaned again, throwing her head back as she pressed into my face. I still had her hands pinned behind her back. She was at my mercy, so I sucked and bit her nipple until she was squirming on my lap, ready to come.

I licked and sucked, and then I let go, pulling back so I could kiss her mouth.

"Miles, I need to…don't stop."

"I won't, not until you ask nicely." I kissed her again before I let go of her hands to run both of mine through her hair and around her body. She wrapped her arms around my neck, pressing her body into me even though she was only partially clothed. She held onto me and ground down on my dick. I let her, knowing I *would* come if we weren't careful. I gripped the back of her neck, keeping her steady as I kissed her, devoured her mouth with mine. I positioned her back against the couch and hovered over her, thrusting slightly against her pussy, even though we were both clothed on our lower halves. The friction was almost too much. She groaned again, so I reached between us and slowly undid the button of her pants.

"Good?" I asked.

"Please, just touch me already."

I grinned and then slid my hand into her panties, swiping my finger over her clit. She was wet, hot. And with that one swipe, she fell over the edge. A single touch of her beautiful pussy, and she came on my hand. I cupped her, sending her further into her orgasm as I delved my fingers between her wet and swollen folds.

She groaned, her body shaking. I leaned down and sucked her nipple into my mouth, and she moaned my name. As she looked at me, coming down off her high, I pulled my hand out of her panties. Meeting her gaze, I licked her wetness off my fingers. She covered her face with her hands, groaning once more, and I grinned.

"So fucking sweet," I said before taking off my glasses so I wouldn't break them and leaning over her.

I didn't go any farther, I knew we weren't ready for that, but I had taken the edge off for her. I'd wait for mine. She held onto me, kissed me again, and then the door opened behind us.

"Hey, did I leave my...?" Tanner's voice trailed off before he smiled widely. "Cool. You and Nessa? It's about time. Sorry for walking in."

Nessa let out a scream and covered herself, even as I blocked Tanner's view of her. He had likely only seen part of her face, but I knew the moment was broken. My dick was still hard, but it wouldn't get touched anytime soon.

"Tanner, get the fuck out."

"Aw, look at you, getting all growly. I'm sorry. Seriously. Sorry." He picked up his book from the table near him and closed the door.

"I could have sworn I locked that," I said, wincing as I leaned down and kissed Nessa's fingers since they were covering her face.

"Did he see anything?" she squeaked.

"No, I'm covering you. You're fine. Let's get you dressed, though."

"I think I'm sort of already dressed. I have no idea how you got my boob out of my shirt like that."

"I'd say practice, but we both know that's not the case." I kissed Nessa again, then helped her dress, willing my dick to calm down.

"So..." she whispered.

"I am sorry about that."

"About making me come? About Tanner? Or what?"

"I'm never going to be sorry about making you come." I couldn't wait to do it again.

"I can't believe I went off that quickly."

"It means I'm going to have to see how long I can tease you next time."

"Oh," she said, her cheeks reddening. "I guess you like the whole tying people up thing? Or just binding? Or like it hard and rough? I can't believe I'm saying this."

I grinned, despite the serious questions. "Sometimes. I don't know, I like it a little rougher, I suppose. But, honestly, with you? I want anything.

Which makes me sound like a cad, but here I am."

"I don't know what I want, Miles. I liked what we did. I'm just not ready for anything more right now."

I nodded, feeling the same, honestly. I leaned down and gripped her hand, pulling her palm to my lips. I kissed her gently, and her eyes darkened.

"You and me? We can do dinner. We can study. We can do what we just did, and however rough you'd like it," I teased, and she swallowed hard.

"I guess we can say we're dating, just not as serious as the others because that's serious. And I'm not ready for that."

I nodded. "Completely understand."

She let out a breath. "We were going to watch a movie." I looked at my dick, and she groaned. "Or maybe I could help take care of that."

I shook my head. "No, we're going to will that little erection of mine away."

"Miles, I don't think there's anything *little* about that," she teased.

And that was the Nessa I knew and liked a lot. The one I'd had a crush on.

"Come here. Cuddle with me, woman."

"Aw, look at you, being all forceful."

I pinched her hip, and she squeaked. "Be careful. That won't be the only thing I pinch."

"Oh, dear God," she said, her eyes darkening more.

"Yes, beware of what you just unleashed."

"Should I make a joke about releasing the Kraken?"

"We already said we weren't going to talk about my dick tonight," I said deadpan, and she snorted. I pulled her onto my lap, kissed her again, and did my best to find a movie, trying not to think about how close she was to my dick.

ELEVEN

Miles

It was amazing how quickly life could change when you weren't ready for it. I lay on the bed, Nessa's knees pressed tightly against my hips, and groaned as she nibbled on my lip.

"This is the best study break ever," she said, grinning, and I leaned back, my hands cradling my head. While I knew I would have rather had them on Nessa, I knew we were both doing our best not to move too quickly. After all, we had said that this wouldn't be forever and that we wanted to maintain our friendship. Sex would change things. That meant the more I touched her, the harder it would be—in every meaning of that phrase.

She rubbed herself against me, and I sucked in a breath, closing my eyes. "You better stop doing that," I said.

She stiffened, a single brow raised. "If I keep going, would it be too much or not enough?"

I rolled my eyes before I turned us both over.

She let out a squeal. "Hey." Now, we were lying side by side, her leg draped over mine as I brushed her hair away from her face. I did my best not to think about what it meant. We were friends, and while I knew she wasn't using me to get over Pacey or even to get over the fear of what had happened with Xander, this still didn't feel real.

One minute, I was pining and pretending that I was okay. The next, she was in my arms, and I wasn't quite sure how that had happened. I needed to stop thinking so hard.

I leaned forward, kissed her on the forehead, and then sat up, draping my arms over my knees as I let out a deep breath.

"Too much, then?" she asked before sitting up next to me. She pressed her leg to mine, but she didn't touch me other than that. It was getting harder to be around her without wanting more. And I didn't mean sex. Sex would be easy between us. I knew that much and figured we would find that out shortly. No, it was everything else that came from it.

Nessa was still worried about school, and we only had a few more days to figure out her plan with that. Then there was grad school for both of us and everything else surrounding those significant decisions. A relationship would get in the way, and I knew that. She knew that. We had been very clear about that. And yet, here we were, our books next to us as we rolled around on my bed, making out and pretending the world wasn't on fire.

"I think we should probably get back to studying."

"We're almost done with my stats homework." She nudged me with her shoulder.

I looked over at her, my lips quirking into a grin. "You're getting better at it."

"I feel like I need to help you study or something. But you've already finished with your English courses, and you got As in those."

I shrugged, my cheeks heating. "I like school. Sorry."

"I was always a decent B and C student in high school. Often, I got As if things worked out right, but it just wasn't my thing. English, though? That was always my jam. Reading and writing and anything having to do with that sort of creativity and deep introspection. That was for me. The math and science part? I mean, I tried, but it just didn't hit me."

"We're not supposed to be good at everything we do."

"So says the guy with the 4.0 GPA in his final year of college."

I swallowed hard. "Some people are just good at school. Other people are good at everything else."

"I'm not good at everything else, either. We both know that."

I frowned. "You shouldn't say that."

"It's the truth. A lot of our friends already know who they want to be and what they want to do with the rest of their lives. I'm still figuring it out."

"Dillon has had how many career changes? And he's our age."

"He found something he likes."

"He had to make changes to make that happen, though. I may know what I want to do in terms of a career, but everything else? I pretty much fail at it all."

She leaned into me again. "Sitting here with you, you don't seem like much of a failure."

If only she knew the mistakes I had made.

I leaned forward, pushing those thoughts from my mind as I brushed her hair from her face. "Let's get some work done and then eat. I know you have a job to do. I have a group project that I need to have a meeting on later, too. I'm so excited."

"That's the one thing I like these days. Most of my projects aren't group-related."

"You would think mine wouldn't be, either. Yet, here I am." I shrugged.

"Let's get to this whole school thing. Yay, statistics." She laughed, and I kissed her again. There was a scuffling noise outside the room, and I stiffened.

"Wait there, let me make sure he's—" Tanner said through my door. I looked up quickly as my parents walked directly into my bedroom, not bothering to knock or to listen to Tanner. Instead, they simply made themselves at home.

I sighed as Nessa squeaked and looked down at herself, making sure she was fully clothed. She was, but any more time with her on my bed, that probably wouldn't have been the case.

My parents met my gaze and then looked over at Nessa before my dad raised his brows, and my mother narrowed her eyes.

"Mom, Dad. What are you doing here?"

Tanner stood behind them, his hands outstretched as he winced.

I met his gaze and shook my head. It wasn't his fault that my parents had walked past him and into the room. Probably the house. They were good at that.

And since they had helped me to pay for my school initially, I couldn't resent them for thinking that they owned part of me. At least, that's what I told myself. Fuck it. I did begrudge them. I'd dealt with my mistakes and paid the price—something I had to keep telling myself.

My parents just looked between Nessa and me, and I sighed before I scooted off the bed and held up my hand. Nessa looked at it, gave me a quick shake of her head, and practically scrambled off the other side of the mattress.

"Mom, Dad, this is Nessa."

"Hi there," Nessa said as she rubbed her palms on her thighs. "It's nice to meet you."

"I think we've seen you around before, right?" my mom asked, her voice not necessarily cool but also not welcoming. I wasn't sure when she had ever been fully accepting of anyone I hung out with. It definitely hadn't been since the accident. She wanted us all in little boxes, safe and tucked away where nobody could hurt us. That just wasn't going to happen.

"Uh, maybe," Nessa began. She gave me a pleading look, and I nodded tightly before holding out my hand. She looked at it again before I leaned forward and took hers, not bothering to wait for her to slide her palm into mine. She was nervous. Hell, so was I. But I wasn't going to let my parents make her feel small. I didn't know what they were here for, but I wouldn't let Nessa get hurt because of their attitudes.

"Anyway, we were just studying," I said. "I think you might've met Nessa before when you came by one night as we were all eating dinner."

"Studying..." Mom began.

Dad cleared his throat. "I remember now—the girls from the other house. Aren't a couple of you dating some of the roommates?" he asked, looking between us.

"It seems like it," I said. "We're all good friends." I squeezed Nessa's hand and gave her a look, and she relaxed slightly. Good. At least one of us could relax somewhat because I was about to scream.

"So, what's going on?" I asked. "Is there a reason you guys decided to barge into my room like this?"

"We're your parents. It's not called barging when we do it." Mom rolled her shoulders back.

"Okay. Nessa? Why don't you go downstairs and give us a minute? Do you mind?"

"If you're sure," she whispered.

I wanted to lean down and kiss her, to rest my lips against hers until she knew everything would be okay. But she was embarrassed enough. I nodded and squeezed her hand, and she quickly walked out, leaving her stuff behind. Even her purse was still in my room, so I knew she wouldn't escape. That was good because I had a feeling I had a lot to explain.

"Seriously?" I asked, sighing. "You can't just barge in on me like that. I'm not a kid anymore, and this is not your home."

"You're still our child," Mom said. "And, seriously, you're going to call that studying? Making out with a girl in your room?"

"Mom. I'm not sixteen. I'm not even a teenager anymore. I'll be twenty-two soon. I'm an adult, and I'm moving to a different state. I'll be looking into the housing market and deciding what my future looks like —things I need to do as an adult. If I want to have a woman in my room, I will. I like Nessa. She's sweet—a good person. You guys embarrassed her. Hell, you embarrassed *me*."

"Watch your language, son," Dad said as he shook his head.

"It's my house. And that's not the point."

"A house we help pay for."

I scoffed. "No, you don't. You helped me the first two years, and I will forever be grateful that you assisted me with school. I would not be where I am without you. But I've been paying for this year. I pay for this house. I'm taking more credit hours than ever to finish on time with my majors. *I'm* doing this, Mom and Dad. I love you both, but you can't just come in whenever you want. I need privacy. I have a life. And I should be able to live it." With those last words, I knew I had said the wrong thing. My mom's face blanched, and I held back a curse. "Mom," I began.

"No, you're right. You are allowed to live your life. It's just the one time we didn't pay attention enough, you almost didn't get to live it, and your sister lost hers. So, I understand. I understand that you think you're an adult now and can make your own decisions, but that's fine. We were just here to check on you because we love you. If you're going to keep pushing us away like this, maybe we need to figure out exactly how you're going to be in Aaron's life."

My dad cursed under his breath, and my eyes widened.

"Wait, you can't just keep Aaron away from me. He's my little brother."

"And Rachelle was your sister. Your twin. We saw how that turned out, didn't we?"

The blow hit me so hard, it was as if she had slapped me. I staggered back, the back of my knees hitting the bed. I sat down, bile filling my mouth.

"Kayla." My dad's tone shocked me. "That was uncalled for."

Tears freely fell down her face. "Maybe, but I'm hurting, too. And he's our son. He doesn't get to push us away. If he's going to act like this, like he did that night, well…maybe he doesn't need to be an influence in Aaron's life. We're going, Parish."

"Kayla," he whispered.

My mother moved away, walking out of my room before my dad gave me a shake of his head and then followed her. I knew I would have to move away. That was just how my career worked. And I knew I would be leaving Aaron behind in a sense, but not this way. Jesus.

"Miles?" Nessa asked from the doorway. I looked up, swallowing hard. She stood there, hugging herself. As I looked at her, I didn't know what to say. She came over to me, then cupped my face and kissed me. I sank into her, needing her taste, just needing *her*. I was grateful when she closed the door behind her. I didn't want anything we said to leave this room. I just needed to breathe to figure out what I was supposed to do.

I needed an anchor, and I couldn't find one. Nessa couldn't be my anchor, but even for a moment, I could pretend.

"I heard part of that. I didn't mean to. I'm sorry, Miles," she whispered.

I looked up at her and swallowed hard. "I think I should probably tell you a couple of things that happened, so what you just saw makes a little more sense."

She frowned. "I don't know if any of that will

make sense. Nothing you could've done deserved that, Miles." I let out a hollow laugh as she sat down next to me. I squeezed her hand, then I stood and started to pace.

"I'm the nerdy brother—the one who liked playing video games and had glasses from the age of six. I was a geek, a nerd. I could've skipped a couple of grades but decided to stay back because of my sister."

She met my gaze, her eyes wide. "Your sister?"

I sighed. "My twin, actually. My twin sister, who didn't get the same grades as I did, skipped class a lot and had a ton more fun than I ever did in high school. Even middle school. She would never skip any grades, and I didn't want to do that without her. So, I stayed behind and took some college classes, some upper-level classes, did extracurricular activities and became a complete nerd. But I always had my sister. No matter what." My heart ached, and I felt it twist. I let out a breath. "She was my best friend, even though she had a hundred other best friends along the way. Her name was Rachelle."

Nessa looked at me, her eyes filling with tears because she had heard the past tense. *She knew.*

"Rachelle was full of life, energetic and brilliant, but school wasn't her thing. My parents never understood that and did their best to help her, but they also never closed her in. They weren't the people you saw today."

Nessa didn't say anything, and for that, I was grateful. I needed to breathe for a moment.

"My sister was a light. A shining light that sometimes dulled just a bit. But when she flared outside of that dullness, she shone on everybody and everything around her. Two days after we graduated high school, I decided that maybe I didn't need to be the lame sibling, who was her twin but felt like the party girl's kid brother in high school. We had both gotten into college, although Rachelle planned to take some community college classes while she figured out what she wanted to do. I was so damn proud of her. She worked her ass off to get in, and she wasn't going to waste money while she found her path. She would forge any path she wanted. And no matter what, she knew that I would always be there for her. Aaron was quite a few years younger than us, and while we bonded with him and he is my baby brother, and I will always be there for him, Rachelle was part of my heart. Yet, after graduation, I decided I just wanted to have some fun. To live life on the other side for a bit and see what my sister did. Learn who she was."

Nessa was crying now, but I didn't touch her. I needed to breathe, and I needed to get through this.

"I had a few drinks. Maybe more than a few. I

ended up getting my stomach pumped because I would've died of alcohol poisoning if I hadn't. I hadn't known when to let up. Everyone around me kept giving me drinks because I was Rachelle's twin; therefore, they assumed I must have the same metabolism as she did when it came to alcohol." I sighed. "That's why I don't drink as much as others do now. I remember what it was like to drink too much. The first time I tasted alcohol, I went too far. I don't even remember getting in the car."

Nessa sucked in a breath, and I swallowed hard.

"I was in the passenger seat. I wasn't driving. Rachelle drove and had the same amount of alcohol in her system as I did, if not more. The first time I had a drink, I let my twin sister drink and drive. We had to get home before Mom and Dad found out. It didn't matter that we were eighteen and newly minted adults. That we had the world in front of us, the rest of our lives to be who we wanted to be and find out who we could be. I don't remember everything from the accident. I *do* remember that Rachelle smiled at me, and I blinked at her, drunk off my ass and unable to do anything but scream when the first bit of metal hit. She hit a guardrail, hadn't even realized she had skidded around a curve. I was wearing my seatbelt. The airbags deployed, and we hadn't been speeding. I had a little bit of internal bleeding that thankfully didn't need surgical intervention. But I'd been covered in bruises and cuts from the glass. I needed a few stitches on my hairline. My wrist and knee got sprained. I walked away to get help."

"Miles," Nessa whispered.

I looked at her then. "It was rote for me to put on my seatbelt when I got in the car. Even drunk, I remembered to do it. Rachelle didn't. In my memories, when we hit the guardrail and metal twisted and glass shattered, I can still see her. Looking over at me as I was in pain, trying to wake up. That isn't what happened. That was a dream or a figment of my imagination or even a drunk hallucination. Rachelle had been thrown through the windshield, face-first through the glass. It broke nearly every bone in her face, cut through her scalp, broke her wrists and her elbow and her collarbone. Glass had punctured her heart, her lungs, and destroyed even more pieces of her. The impact killed her instantly. They told me later that with the booze in her system and given the speed of the accident, she likely hadn't felt a thing. Everything happened so fast, I don't even think she felt fear. I hope to hell that's the truth. My twin sister died the first night I had a drink. The first time I wasn't there to protect her how I always had."

I let out a breath and wiped away the single tear that had fallen. "I loved her so fucking much. Still do.

We both made mistakes that night, but I walked away, and she didn't. My parents haven't forgiven me."

It felt as if I'd run a marathon. My heart raced, and I couldn't catch up. It was all out now. Everything. All of my secrets.

No more hiding my mistakes.

"Miles. I'm so sorry. I don't know what to say." She let out a breath. "It wasn't your fault. They lost her, but they could've lost you, too."

I sucked in a breath. "You're right. My parents twisted their grief into overprotectiveness. They love me. I don't think they'll ever trust me the same way, but maybe I deserve that."

"Miles..." she began.

I shook my head. "No, there are reasons we're not supposed to be those people and make those choices. I get that. I wasn't an adult for more than a minute when I decided to have that drink. I made a choice. Same as my sister. My parents are overprotective and pushy, and they're so afraid if they let go of the reins for one instant that I'll die as she did. They're so afraid that Aaron will see the path Rachelle was on, the night I made the worst choice of my life, and follow me down into that dark hole, as well. I see their decisions, and I understand why they do the things they do, even if I can't change it. So, that is why I'm the geeky kid with the overprotective parents who want to wrap him in Bubble Wrap and make his lunch for him. They haven't let up since the accident, and they probably never will. I need to find a way to make that work. Because that's who I am. The night I made the worst decision of my life, my sister died. My twin. And yet, here I am."

I let out a shaky breath, and then Nessa was there, holding me tightly. I had never told a single person that entire story, and I wasn't sure I could ever do it again. Nessa held me, her tears warm and wet against my chest as I wrapped my arms around her.

I didn't know what this meant or what it should mean. I had to stop looking for answers in the future when I couldn't even find them in the present.

So, I simply held Nessa and pretended. I pretended that I was okay. That things made sense.

I pretended that maybe this wouldn't be the ending before it had even begun.

I did what I was good at. I pretended.

Twelve

Nessa

Three days later, my heart still physically ached for Miles. I'd known he had some kind of trauma in his past—it seemed we all did—but I hadn't known the guilt that lay shrouded beneath.

I tried to figure out what I should do or say to make him see that I would be there for him—as friends and whatever else we were. In reality, I knew I needed to be there for him in any way I could.

"Now, what are you thinking about?" Natalie asked as she looked up at me. I blinked and realized that my roommates were all staring at me, and I was looking off into the distance, thinking about Miles.

"Sorry." I didn't want to break his confidence and tell them the source of my worry, but it wasn't easy. "Letting my thoughts wander."

"About Miles?" Natalie asked as she leaned forward.

I sighed. "Maybe." I didn't want to get into too much detail.

"I'm so happy that you and he are finally starting a relationship." Elise and Mackenzie shared a look.

"What do you mean by *finally*?" I asked, frowning.

"It just seems like you guys get along well," Mackenzie said slowly, and I knew she was holding back a wince.

"We do. And we're friends. It's not like we slept together yet," I added.

"Why the hell not?" Natalie asked before she threw up her hands at our looks. "Hi. Yes, I am the resident virgin, but that doesn't mean I believe that sex is wrong, and we shouldn't have it. I would love to have sex someday. I just need to meet a guy I wouldn't mind touching me."

"We all know that you don't mind Miles touching you," Elise added with a wink in my direction.

I rolled my eyes. "You're right; I don't. Only I don't want to ruin anything by having sex too quickly. So, we're waiting. Things won't be all roses and angels and everything with the future. He's moving soon, and I don't know what I'll be doing."

"You're not dropping out," Mackenzie said, narrowing her eyes.

I sighed and held up my hands. "I know, I won't. At least, not this semester."

"Then that means you only have one more semester to worry about," Elise said.

"We're working on those scholarships. You're going to make it."

I nodded, grateful for my friends. I would make it. At least, that's what I kept telling myself. My friends were fantastic people who helped me with grants and made sure I could make it through the last semester. I would be okay, at least I thought I would. Not entirely because I didn't know what I wanted to do with the rest of my life, seeing as things kept changing, but I knew that Miles wasn't my forever.

"So, it's not forever with you and Miles," Natalie began, and we both ignored how Mackenzie and Elise scowled at us. "As I was saying, it's not forever. But it can be for right now. We're allowed that. I mean, I would love right now," she said, winking.

"Right now would be wonderful..." Mackenzie began.

I cut in. "I don't know what's going to happen in

the future, but I am having fun. And I'm going to say it to remember that."

"Good. So, have fun. And when you're ready, have amazing sex because I have a feeling that Miles may surprise us all." Mackenzie winked, and we all laughed, even though I knew I was blushing from head to toe.

"What's that look for?" Elise pointed at me.

Mackenzie narrowed her eyes. "It seems she might know a little bit more about Miles than she's letting on."

"I'm not saying anything," I whispered.

That in and of itself said enough. I remembered how he had held me, the way he touched me just the right way. I knew Miles could take off those glasses and be into some kinky goodness, and I wasn't sure exactly what I would do with that—other than enjoy myself.

"Not to bring the tone of this down, but have you gotten another present or anything lately?" Mackenzie asked.

I shook my head, my stomach aching. "No, which I'm grateful for. Hopefully, it was just a one-time thing or something. It was really bizarre."

Elise frowned. "I know. It's worrying. But we're here if you need us."

I nodded, relief and nervousness warning inside me. "I know that. And, hopefully, I don't get any more flowers. This whole thing doesn't make sense. Like the fact that he clung so quickly. We didn't even have two full dates."

"Hopefully, it's over, and you don't have to think about it again. I hate that you had to deal with it at all," Mackenzie added.

"On the surface, Xander seemed like such a nice guy. But maybe those are the ones you need to worry about," Natalie said, frowning.

"Maybe. Although *your* guys aren't jerks," I said, looking over at them.

Elise shook her head. "They aren't. They expect us to like them just because we're nice to them. If that makes sense."

"Exactly. Miles is a good man, but not the quintessential *nice guy* if *that* makes sense."

"It does, totally. And it would be nice if the other three could rub off on their jerk roommate," Natalie grumbled, and everyone else looked at me. I just shrugged.

I didn't know what was going on between Tanner and Natalie, but I knew there wasn't any love lost there. They were always growly towards one another, and while it may look like attraction to some, I wasn't so sure. Natalie didn't seem flustered; she just seemed…annoyed.

"When do you have to go back to work?"

Mackenzie asked as we went through our homework, trying to get caught up for the week.

"I work tomorrow, and then I have a meeting with my professor to go over different jobs I can have for those grants. I don't want to have to drop out next semester, but I just don't know how I'm going to pay for it." I looked up at the girls. "And nobody gets to help me like that."

Natalie shrugged. "You know my parents would help out."

"Yes, I know. And while I'd be grateful, things would change between us, and I don't want that."

"I understand, but I also want you to be able to finish school so you can have your degree and begin what you need to do next."

"We're figuring it out." Somehow. "At least, we've decided that I'm staying for this semester since I already paid for it, and there's no use trying to wait for a refund." I hated that I was so worried about money that I couldn't sleep, but I couldn't focus on anything else right now. I needed to concentrate on work, school, and Miles.

I liked Miles. It wasn't like I was waiting for love to have sex with him. I was simply waiting for trust. Was that it? Or maybe I was holding out for a promise that I knew would never come. Therefore, I didn't have to worry about getting hurt.

I trusted Miles. I always had, though I had always thought of him as only a friend. It was such a complicated mess that sometimes I just wanted to bury myself and forget that I could be my own worst enemy.

I honestly didn't know why I was waiting anymore. I knew it might have started as me trying to play it safe, and both of us not wanting to hurt each other when we knew we had to walk away at the end of the year. Only that might not be the case anymore. I would likely get hurt no matter what. He would hurt me, just like I would hurt him. I already liked him enough as a friend, *and* as something more. Things were going to hurt.

Somehow, I needed to find a way to make that manageable.

So why wasn't I sleeping with the guy I kept dreaming about and wanted?

I let out a breath and then pushed those thoughts from my mind to focus on my friends. That was the least I could do, even while everything else was falling apart around me.

I opened the door and smiled as Miles walked in. He leaned down to brush his lips to mine. I leaned into him, taking a deep breath as I did my best not to wrap my arms around him and never let him go.

"Hey there." He brushed my hair from my face.

"Hi. I just finished work, and now I'm working on grant proposals and should probably get some homework done." I sighed.

He nodded and kissed me again. "I'm here for stats homework, and I have to go through a few of my labs."

"Is that the one with the carbon paper?" I asked.

He shook his head. "Right now, I'm on grid paper. And then I need to write an actual paper from it. I don't do carbon paper anymore since that's a first-year lab."

"See? I had to take a lab for one of my core classes, and I feel like I don't know what I'm doing."

"You do. Didn't you get like a B+ in that? You did great."

"I did. I don't remember sleeping much during it, though."

"I'm now one of the TAs for a gen-ed lab, and it's not as fun as it was when I took the class."

"There are so many things wrong with that sentence." I laughed as I looked up at him. He was so freaking cute sometimes. "First, you had fun?"

"Yes. I'm a nerd, remember?"

"You're a hot one," I corrected, and he rolled his eyes.

"Thanks for that."

"I didn't know you were a TA, did I?"

He tilted his head as he looked at me. "You did. It's the class I do on Fridays."

"Oh. Right. I knew that. Sorry."

"It's fine. I never talk about it since it's barely any stipend, and it's only so I can afford to do a few things other than pay my rent."

"It's good that you have a job, though." I leaned into him as we walked.

"Thanks for that," he said with a laugh. "Hey, you're working at a bookstore. I'm working in a lab that somehow, somewhat has to do with my job. It's a living."

"Yes. And, hopefully, my professor will be able to help me find another job that pays a little more."

"You'd quit the bookshop?" he asked as I led him to my bedroom.

I shook my head. "Not necessarily. More like I'd get a second job."

"Jesus, Nessa. Are you going to have time to sleep?"

"I can sleep while standing up. Maybe. I don't know if I'm going to have much choice at this point."

"I'm here if you need me. You know that." He sat next to me on my bed, and I swallowed hard.

"I know. And it's kind of nice knowing that."

"Are you ready for the fun to begin?" he asked as he opened my textbook.

"Hell, we're studying hell," I said on a laugh and leaned into him as he started looking over some of my formulas.

"You've got this."

"You'd think so, but this took me forever. I don't know why I have to take this stupid class," I grumbled and then held up my hand before he could tell me exactly why I was taking the stupid class.

"I don't know if I want to know, so let's just pretend," I said with a laugh.

"Okay, we can pretend. Let's go over a couple of these that you skipped, and then we can play strip-studying." I looked up at him then, a smile on my face. "Strip-studying?"

"What? Dillon said he and Elise enjoy playing it. I figured we might, too."

"We're going to play strip-studying just because they like it?" I asked, laughing now.

"I think we'll enjoy playing it because I want to see you naked," he growled low.

I looked up at him and swallowed hard.

"You know, I think I'm going to like that kind of studying." I laid my book on the bed and leaned over to slowly take off his glasses.

"That's going to make it a little difficult for me to see you," he said as he leaned down and kissed me again.

"Well, then, I guess you'll just have to do it by touch," I teased, wondering where those words had come from. I wasn't good at this, usually. Although I was better at it when I wrote certain scenes. When I had time to think about what I should say, things made sense.

He smiled at me and nipped my lip before deepening the kiss. Somehow, he was over me, kissing me softly as I moaned. I was ready for this, had been since the first time we had spoken about it, even though I had told myself I needed time.

I knew I was going to get hurt no matter what, so I might as well live in the moment.

I liked Miles. Watching him walk away would devastate me, but this moment could make it all worth it. I would make sure of that. So, I leaned in and kissed him again. He slowly let his hands roam all over my body, and I raked my fingers down his back as he groaned before deepening the kiss once more and slowly rocking against me, his jean-clad cock hard against my heat. I swallowed hard and then let out a gasp when he tugged my arms above my head, clasping them together in one hand.

"Are you good?" he asked, his gaze on mine. I knew he could see me this close. His glasses were helpful for distance. We wouldn't need them for this, but I nodded anyway. "Yes. Please."

"Whatever you want," he whispered, and then he kissed me again, and I was lost. He tugged at my shirt, nibbling my stomach before pulling down my bra slightly to suck on my breast. My nipple puckered, turning to a hard little nub against his tongue as he took his time and nearly sent me over the edge. I keened, rocking against him. Needing him.

He hummed, the slight scrape of his beard a new sensation that made me wetter. He sat up and pulled off his shirt, and my mouth dropped open, watering at the sight. He was all hard lines and ridges, and I couldn't help but want to reach out and touch him. He shook his head, took his shirt, and slowly wrapped it around my wrists. My eyes widened, and he grinned. "Are you still good?"

"Yes," I breathed, surprising myself with the need in my voice.

Miles' eyes darkened before he leaned down and kissed me hard, tugging my hands back over my head, still tied together by his shirt. It was loose enough that I could get free quickly if needed, but knowing that he was the one in control just then? It was almost too much. It was so good. So much rode me, and I had so many decisions to make, answers I didn't have. But letting Miles take control right now was everything.

He kissed me harder before letting go of my arms,

but I kept them in place, knowing that was what he wanted me to do.

"Good girl," he whispered before undoing the clasp on my bra and letting my breasts fall. He kissed them, paying special attention to them and pressing them together as he slowly bit and sucked. I knew I would be sore tomorrow; minor bruises all over my body that would be from the most marvelous sensations of my life.

He pressed against me harder as he leaned up, and then he moved back in, nibbling my stomach and coming to rest against the top of my pants. I groaned, pressing my thighs together, but he pulled off my leggings and panties in one go, shocking a gasp out of me. Before I could even breathe in and think too hard about it, his mouth was between my legs, and he was sucking at me, licking my pussy. I groaned, rocking my hips. He pushed me down, keeping me steady so he was the one in control. I groaned again, trying my best to remember to keep my arms back.

He spread my folds and licked me, diving his tongue deep into my pussy as he breathed cool air over my clit. Then he sucked and licked, his fingers there, and I could barely breathe.

I came hard on his face and his hand, wondering how it had even begun. Before I could think, he kissed my pussy again and then flipped me to my stomach.

He smacked my ass, a quick sting before kissing where he had touched. I sucked in a breath, the sensations making me even wetter. I pushed my ass into his face, and he spread my cheeks, licking me from behind in ways no one had ever done before. I groaned, arching into him as he ate at me before I came again. And then his fingers were between my thighs, and I was panting his name, my whole body shaking.

I looked over my shoulder and groaned as he stood there naked, his cock in his hand, thick and long and rigid. I watched as he slowly slid a condom over his length, and then he was behind me again.

"Tell me you're ready," he said, and I nodded. "I need the words, babe."

I shivered at his tone and swallowed hard. "Please, get inside me."

"Anything you want," he said, and then he was there, the tip of his dick right at my entrance. With my gaze on his over my shoulder, he speared me, thrusting so hard in one movement that I came again, my pussy clamping around his cock. He groaned, squeezed my hips, and then one hand moved to my breast, the other dropping near my head as he clenched the bedsheets. He pumped into me, faster and harder. Both of us panted, and I could barely keep up, but all I wanted to do was gasp and try to stay in the moment. I couldn't think. Couldn't breathe. I couldn't do anything. Then, his fingers trailed over my clit, and I came once more, surprising myself. I had never come so many times in one session. I couldn't even focus. He pounded into me again, and then he pulled out of me. It left me bereft, but then the t-shirt was off my arms, and I was on my back. He slammed into me one more time, groaning as he kissed me, coming hard and deep inside me.

He was so gentle, even with the forcefulness of our lovemaking. I could barely keep up, but I didn't want to. He held me as we came down from our highs, and I knew that even though this had been the most miraculous moment of my life, it had been a mistake, as well.

We both knew we'd have to walk away after this. There could be no forever for us.

However, at that moment, I couldn't care. Not when he took such good care of me, didn't stop touching me, and wouldn't stop looking at me. I snuggled against him, let my eyes drift shut, and pretended.

I told myself I could believe that this was more than just a night. More than just a touch.

I let myself *be*. If only for a moment.

Thirteen

Nessa

I leaned back and stretched, my eyes going bleary. I'd worked on this project for most of the day, and all I wanted to do was go back to bed. Unfortunately, that wasn't going to happen anytime soon. I had class, meetings after, and work later.

At some point, time permitting, I hoped to see Miles, but I didn't know if that would happen. Not when he was even busier than me. He had a complicated group project in lab coming up that stressed him out. Both of us were doing our best not to talk about the fact that we weren't sure what would happen next semester.

I pushed those thoughts from my mind and made my way to the living room. I was alone in the house, the girls either at work, school, or with their guys—in other words, off living their lives. I finally looked at the clock and held back a curse. I needed to get going. I quickly stuffed my books into my bag, put my work shirt on top, and looked around to make sure I had everything.

I wasn't dressed for a date or time with Miles, and part of me figured that might be a good thing. Things were getting a little too serious—not that I was surprised. Sex made things serious, even if we'd only joked about it before.

It would always be serious with him. No matter how hard we tried to keep it casual, I couldn't *stop* wanting more when it came to Miles.

Only, we were both moving. I might be leaving even earlier than either of us had planned. I had to get a real job and become an adult and figure out what to do with the rest of my life. I wouldn't be able to do it making plans that could go up in smoke in an instant. Plans were more Mackenzie's thing, and even when everything had been derailed in her life, she had found a way to make it right. I would have to do the same.

I looked at my phone and smiled, a text from Miles lighting up the screen.

Miles: *Thinking of you. Miss you.*

I smiled.

Me: *Miss you too.*

My stomach roiled a bit, thinking about what might happen when we had to walk away. We both knew there wasn't a future for us. That meant I had to stop fretting over every single decision when it came to him.

I looked at my text and frowned when I noticed that Miles was on two lines in my messages. As if he had started a new chat with me with his most recent text. I needed to update my phone. Maybe that was why it was bugging out. The cell had been doing that often lately, randomly chirping and ringing once before it powered down. I needed to get a new one, but that wouldn't happen anytime soon. This baby needed to last me a long while because even some of my schoolwork required a smartphone. As did a few of my grant ideas.

I also wrote a few chapters on my notes app that I would send to my computer to edit before adding them to my book. It was my lifeline, and I hated that it seemed to be acting up.

I shook my head and made my way to campus. I had statistics class first and took as many notes as possible, even though my head ached and my hand hurt. I ignored that pain. It wasn't as bad as it used to be. Since Miles had started helping me, something had started to click. I would never be a mathematician, nor would I get an A in the class, but I figured I was learning some things, at least, and I wasn't as bad off as I had been. That counted as a win in my book. And anything to increase my GPA meant I was happy. The schools I was looking at for grad school, if I could get in at all, needed me to stay at my current GPA. I didn't have Miles' 4.0, but my grades were better now than they had been in high school. Thankfully.

I had another class later this afternoon, but I needed to meet with my dad first. I'd been planning on a phone call, but he had texted me during class. Thankfully, my phone was on silent, even though it was flaking out. I was supposed to meet him at our favorite coffee shop. A place on campus that had two floors and was where everybody always seemed to be. Dillon had met Elise there, though the two hadn't spoken at the time. Mackenzie had had a couple of interactions within its walls that I knew people still talked about, as well, even though they weren't as important to her these days.

I didn't do much at the coffee shop other than drink cheap coffee—which wasn't easy to do with most of their prices.

I found my dad sitting in a corner, his glasses perched on the tip of his nose. He looked a little dubious, sitting there surrounded by a bunch of students who were my age or younger. This probably wasn't the best place for us to have this conversation, but he had chosen it, so we were going with it.

I looked at him and waved. His whole face brightened when he saw me. My heart did that little clutching thing it did, and I couldn't help but lean into the emotions because my dad didn't smile like that often anymore. I had lost my mother, but he had lost his wife. Now, a seemingly instant, insurmountable mountain of bills and grief had tackled us until we were drowning and unable to crawl our way out of the abyss. Still, my dad was there for me. He was my rock. He hadn't pushed me away or tried to put me in a box. He had stepped back ever so slightly to watch me grow and help me plant my feet firmly in the soil so I could bloom into the woman I needed to be. Yet, I wasn't there yet. I was not that woman. I wasn't sure when I might find her because I was not my mother's daughter. I was not my father's daughter. I was not Miles' girlfriend. I was no one but myself, and I didn't know who that person was.

As I stood in the middle of a coffee shop as people milled around me, smiling or stressed or dealing with emotional turmoil and their day-to-day lives, I had my existential crisis. I wondered who I could be in front of a man who had cared for me, no matter the choices I made. He had pushed me to become the woman I wanted to be, even though I wasn't sure who that was.

My father tilted his head as he studied me, and I had a feeling he knew exactly where my mind had gone. Perhaps not down a path of crisis, but at least the idea that I would think about so many things all at once and end up with a blank expression. He shook his head and stood up, holding out his hands. I moved around others, trying not to bump into anyone as I made my way to my father. I took his hand in mine and then reached around with my other arm and hugged him tightly. I wasn't in middle school or even high school, shying away from my parents' affections. I had lost my mother, and there was no getting her back. There would be no more instances of holding my mother and telling her that I loved her and missed her.

There'd be no more time spent trying to pretend that I was okay becoming the person I was without her here to watch. I wouldn't shy away from my dad's embrace. Nor would I dwell on the times I had because of the person I'd thought I needed to become.

"It's good to see you," my dad said, and I hugged him tightly again before reaching back around him to straighten his sweater.

"You're looking nice. Are these new glasses?" I asked.

"They are. It was time for a change. My prescription's the same, but one of the lenses on my previous ones was a little wobbly. I had to let them go."

Those had been my mother's favorite glasses, the ones he had worn for so long and had finally broken. I knew that he thought about it, but we wouldn't talk about it. We were good at that. Not talking. At least, that's what I thought. Now, we needed to speak, even with the customers around us.

I recognized a few people, Mackenzie's ex-boyfriend was in the corner with his new girlfriend, but he didn't pay any attention to me. I was fine with that. It didn't matter much. Even Dillon's ex-girlfriend was here, milling about. Our friend, Sasha, also walked around. She gave me a little wave before going back to her boyfriend.

I recognized so many people from school and parties, but my roommates weren't here. Not the family I had chosen and made. For that, I was grateful. If I broke down, I didn't want them to see.

My dad reached out and squeezed my hand. "I love you, hon. I know you're not sleeping well because of seemingly insurmountable issues, but you need to know that we're going to be okay."

I sat next to him in the booth, close enough that

our voices could be low, even though nobody was paying attention to us. My dad had already bought me coffee, but it sat in front of me untouched, still hot.

"Are we going to lose the house?"

"It's looking that way," my dad said. My heart broke, another twist that shattered everything I was. "Some of the debt from the hospital backed up some bills when I had to take time off. And, yes, school. The house will cover most of it."

"I can take next semester off. Take a break. Get a full-time job. Everly can give me more hours. She's already talked to me about it, even though she wasn't too thrilled about the idea."

"You're not doing that."

"I have to. I have a meeting with my professor after this. I'm getting a better job next semester in addition to the bookstore. Maybe we can make that work for a little bit longer than planned."

"Nessa, darling, you have enough for your last semester. That's not something you need to worry about."

"Dad—"

"Don't. I'm here because I wanted to see you on campus. And I wanted to see you in this world of yours that you love. You are so brilliant, and I cannot wait to see how you shine outside of this. We all decided—you, me, and your mother—that you would go to a smaller school, one that was still a state-run college so you could get better scholarships and wouldn't make us go broke after a single year. We made that decision, even though you could have gotten into a more expensive school."

I started. "My grades weren't that great, Dad."

"They were good enough for those bigger schools. Maybe not Ivy League, but bigger schools. More expensive ones. We took a chance and went with this one. And you're thriving. *Keep* thriving. You're so close to the end. I'm so proud of you."

"Dad, the house..."

"The house is paid for. We wouldn't be losing the house to the bank. I would sell it to pay for the rest of the bills. This is what happens with our medical system and insurance. It is a horrible way for our society to live, but we are privileged in that you can still go to school, and I can still keep my job, even if I have to downsize. The fact that I'm even holding onto a home that's far too big for me is a privilege, Nessa. Things are tight, and they will be for a while, but I'm an adult. You don't need to put this on yourself."

I swallowed hard, my eyes stinging. "I have dreams, Dad. But I also have reality."

"You do not need to put your dreams on hold for me. Your mother wouldn't want that."

"That's a low blow," I whispered.

"Maybe, but it's exactly what we need. I love you, daughter of mine. I love you with every ounce of my soul. Your mother did, too. You will finish school. You will disappoint me if you don't."

I winced, my heart aching. "Dad, really? You're going there?"

"You bet I am. I'm going to throw down the parental gauntlet if you disappoint me. You would also disappoint your mother."

"Dad," I gasped.

"It's the truth. You wanted school. These are your dreams. We never forced you to make this choice, so you are not finishing school to make us happy. You would be doing it to make yourself happy. I know it might seem easier to take a break right now so you can pay for this last semester, but that's not the case. If I have to sell the house to finish paying off the bills for those experimental treatments, I will. I will live in a small, dilapidated apartment, and I will start a new life. We've had to start over before, and I will do it again. You are my daughter, and you will not put your dreams on hold for me."

"I don't want you to have to give up things in life." My dad squeezed my shoulders, and I reached out to wipe away a tear.

"I am not giving up anything. We are making the choices we need to make as adults. You will find your path. You want to be an English professor and teach the worlds of literature that people can dive into and find new places in? That is what you need to do. You have a book written that you want to publish? Do it. Be that person. I know some people out there say that you should go to college for a degree that will earn you large amounts of money and focus on just that. That may work for them, but that's not for us. You are reasonable, you are forceful in your intentions, and you are creative. Creative people need an outlet. You are one of those. Write, teach, create. Be the Nessa that I know and love. Thrive. Don't give up your dreams for me."

I swallowed hard. "I love you," I whispered.

"I love you, too. Now, let's drink our coffee before it gets cold, and you can tell me all about this boy in your life."

I froze. "Boy?"

"I didn't want to look, but I'm pretty sure that's a hickey on your neck," he drawled, and I winced.

"Oh, God."

"Yes. Let's just discuss his name and his address so I can beat him up."

"Dad!" I laughed.

"Fine, what's his name?"

"His name is Miles."

Dad frowned. "Miles? As in one of the roommates? Pacey's roommate?"

"There's nothing with Pacey and me."

"I know. Though he is a nice guy."

"He is the greatest. And he's not mine. I'm okay with it." Even as I said that, I knew it was true. My dad just smiled.

"That's good to hear. Tell me about this Miles. Is he nice? Does he buy you flowers?"

"Dad," I said. "Only one man in my life buys me flowers." That made me think of Xander, and I held back a shudder. I did not want to think about him. He hadn't contacted me since, and even though they weren't doing much about it, the campus police were trying.

"Who? You're dating more than one boy?"

I looked up at my dad and frowned. "I was talking about you. The yellow roses and the daisies?"

Dad just blinked at me. "I don't remember giving you flowers, baby."

I swallowed hard and smiled, shaking my head. Everything went cold, and I tried to catch my breath. "Sorry, I must be thinking about someone else."

"Nessa?"

"Anyway, let's talk about Miles." I proceeded to tell him all about Miles, did my best not to think about the fact that the first time Xander had sent me something, it had been the day he attacked me. I had thought the flowers were from my dad, but Xander must have written my dad's name.

I tried not to think about it, but I would have to call the police again, at least the person I had been working with, so they had notes. But I didn't have evidence, and it likely wouldn't be enough.

I tried not to let that get me down, tried not to do anything that made me feel as if I were failing. But I was. Xander had sent me flowers, and he had hurt me. But he hadn't done anything since. So, maybe I needed to stop stressing about it. Or, at the very least, stop dwelling on it. Because I couldn't do anything but try to be safe.

After I met with Dad, I saw my professor, although she didn't have much to say about the new job. Mostly, she said they were still looking, and that I should be able to get one soon. In other words, I would have a decent TA job on top of my bookstore job for the last semester, and I'd find a way to make it work. I wouldn't be sleeping, and I would only see Miles in passing, but it would be fine.

Besides, it wouldn't matter because it wasn't like Miles and I were forever anyway.

I made it through my last class and then headed home—the first one home for some reason. There was a note on the fridge. Mackenzie and Elise were having dinner at Dillon's brother's bar, and I sighed since Natalie was with her parents for the evening. It looked like I'd be alone again. Miles wouldn't even be here.

We didn't need to be together every minute, though it sometimes felt as if we weren't together at all.

I pulled out my phone to text him to see what he was doing. I missed him. We had both said we would live the time we had together to its fullest, and that's what we would do. Phone in hand, I got an alert for an email from my agent. My pulse raced, and I opened it.

Another rejection. That made ten. Ten rejections on a book I loved that still hadn't found a home. I knew some of my favorite authors had gotten hundreds of rejections. This was just part of the routine. But after today, it hurt. It fucking hurt.

I texted Miles because I would pretend that everything was fine. That I wasn't breaking inside. That I wasn't floundering.

If I pretended, I could give him my books and find fiction that made sense.

Me: *Hey there.*

Miles: *Hey there. Class go okay?*

I lay on my bed and got under the covers, holding my phone close as I looked down at it. I didn't even realize I was crying until the tears wet my pillow.

Me: *I had a pretty good day. I'm rocking stats.*

Miles: *That's good. Wish I was there. I have this stupid group project meeting for another hour. Maybe I can stop by after?*

It would probably be silly for him to come over since I didn't have much time before bed, but then again, I needed to see him.

I just wanted to see Miles, to pretend that everything was okay.

Me: *Come on over. I'll let you in as soon as you're here.*

Miles: *Sounds like a plan. Miss you, babe.*

I smiled and held the phone close before I texted back.

Me: *Miss you too, babe.*

I looked down at the phone and tried to be okay. I would find a way. Somehow.

Miles made me happy. I would lean on him, even if it hurt to think about what would happen next semester.

FOURTEEN

Miles

I walked into the house and nodded at Pacey and Dillon as Pacey glared at his homework, and Dillon stared at his.

"Everything okay?" I asked, raising a brow.

Pacey scowled even harder. "Yes, just having trouble with this one."

"I'd ask if I could help, but I'm the science geek. You're the math one." Pacey flipped him off, and Dillon just cackled. "Pacey is doing physics homework, so I'm pretty sure he's the science *and* math geek."

"And proud of it. Usually," Pacey grumbled. "I'm

just not wrapping my head around this, but I will. I need to let it click. And coffee. Coffee helps everything."

"Coffee sounds great. I'm cold," I said as I took off my coat.

"I don't understand how there are random cold fronts and icy weather at all times of the year in this state," Dillon said as he leaned his head back.

"It's because you got spoiled being out in California for so long," I said. "Now, you have to suffer through all four seasons."

"Sometimes in a day," Pacey said.

"At least, we have sun here. Unlike your old home," I added.

Pacey shrugged. "Touché. Okay, coffee and homework. Sounds like exam time."

"Nessa should be here soon. She had an afternoon shift with Everly and wanted some help with her stats homework."

"Is that what we're calling it these days?" Pacey asked, waggling his brows.

"Stop it," I said, my ears turning red.

"What? You guys seem happy. You are happy, right? Nessa's my friend, and I will kick your ass if you're not making her happy."

Maybe if it had been anyone else, a tiny kernel of jealousy would have filled me. It couldn't, though, not with Pacey. At first, when the whole Pacey and Nessa thing had exploded last year, I'd been pissed off at Pacey. Not because of Nessa's crush and her feelings for him, but more so that Pacey hadn't seen it. He hadn't done anything about it until it was almost too late.

That had annoyed me to no end. And I said something about it. It had been the only time I'd ever stood up to Pacey because Pacey wasn't the kind of person I needed to stand up to most days. Only Pacey had hurt Nessa, even if by accident. And though I hadn't been a part of the situation at the time, I still hadn't wanted to see her get hurt.

Things were better now, and I knew there were no feelings there, so the fact that Pacey was so overprotective was almost something nice—a boon rather than something overbearing and domineering. At least, that's what I told myself. I would not be telling Nessa that. She would kick both our asses, and we would probably deserve it.

"Nessa and I are taking things slow," I said after a minute, taking a sip of my coffee.

"Slow," Dillon said, shaking his head. "Seriously? That's what you're going with?"

"Yes, slow. Things are different between us than they were with you and Elise and Mackenzie. I'll be leaving soon. I only have a semester and a half left, and then I'm gone. And though we might have next semester figured out with her and school, she will be leaving soon, too. And we don't know where yet. None of us do."

"It's odd to think that some of you guys will be moving out of state."

Pacey cleared his throat. "Mackenzie and I are both applying to Oxford, by the way," he said, almost too casually.

My eyes widened. "You mean you guys would be leaving the country?"

"If we find programs that work. We're going to try to find a place together, and with our majors and the programs we want, that means we'll have to focus on some of the bigger schools that have programs big enough for both of us."

"Hell," Dillon said, shaking his head.

"You guys can't just leave," I said, and then I laughed.

"You're leaving, as well," Pacey said.

"Elise and I are staying here," Dillon said after a minute. "We're thinking about finding a place together. You know, after the school year."

I just smiled. "You know that's not an actual announcement or a surprise, right?" I asked, and Pacey laughed.

"The two of you fit. There's no going back to something less serious."

"The girls are here often enough, and you guys are at the girls' house enough that you're practically living together *now*."

"True, but it'll be different. You know?" Dillon asked, shaking his head. "But we're staying in Denver."

"Of course, you are. Your degrees and jobs make sense for that. And you have the big family businesses you're going to be working towards. It makes total sense."

"You and Nessa won't be finding a place together?" Pacey said.

"We've only been together for a few weeks." Though it felt like longer in some respects. I just didn't allow myself to think too hard about that.

"Hell, it's odd to think we're not going to be like this next year. That we'll all be in different places."

"Colorado is still my home. I want to move back once I finish grad school. If I can get a job out here, I want to be near my brother." And my parents, but I didn't say that. Mostly because it was hard to think about them without feeling as if they were honing in.

"For however long you have, just take care of her," Pacey said after a moment, and I nodded. "That's my goal. And now, I'm going to get a few snacks and head up to my room. If I don't hear the doorbell, can you send her up?" I asked, and Pacey nodded.

"Of course. After I question her about her motives with you, much like I'm doing with you right now."

I rolled my eyes. "Please, don't do that. You're going to scare her away."

"Nessa's made of sterner stuff than that," Dillon said.

"I don't know," Pacey said. "Not that she isn't strong, but she does frighten quite easily."

"That's enough of that," I said, shaking my head. I made a quick cheese and vegetable plate and then headed up to my room, books in hand.

I was just getting settled when the door opened, and Nessa walked in.

"Oh, good, you have snacks," she said as she put her things down on the small table in the corner and came to sit next to me on the couch. She kissed me softly, and I leaned forward, deepening the kiss slightly. She sighed and leaned into me.

"Hi there," she whispered.

"Hi back. Let me feed you."

"You sure do like taking care of me," she said as she pulled away slightly to pick up a cube of cheese.

"Of course, I do. I kind of like you." I leaned into her again, kissing her softly and doing my best to hold back and not move too quickly.

She smiled and then leaned back, picking up another cube of cheese. "I like that you take care of me, though." She gave me a warm look, and I figured that was as good as we would get, talking about our feelings and who we were to each other. Talking about it too much would only make us remember that this wasn't permanent. Not that any relationship was guaranteed, but especially in college, ours had an actual expiration date. I purposely didn't want to think about that.

I nipped at her lip, and she grinned.

"So, I guess we're supposed to be studying?" she asked, and I sighed.

"Yes, for now. Later? Just you wait."

"That sounds like a plan to me," she said and bent over the table to pick up her books.

"You're getting this," I said after we finished the first sets of problems for her homework.

"Finally. I'm going to have to thank you for this later."

She blushed, and I chuckled. "Yes, you should."

"I meant like baking you something."

"Sure. With all this time you have," I said dryly.

She winced. "It's only going to get worse next semester if I get that TA job."

"You can make it work. You may need to sleep while standing up, but you can make it work."

"I hope so. My dad sort of laid into me, thinking about dropping out."

My brows rose. "You didn't tell me about what your dad said. I knew you talked to him, but I didn't want to ask."

"It's not good. But my dad is amazing." She went on to tell me exactly what he had said, and I leaned forward and kissed her gently.

"Your dad sounds pretty amazing."

"I know. I'm lucky to have him, even though what we might lose sucks."

"You'll gain so much because you have each other. And now I sound like I just rolled right off of a Hallmark movie film truck."

"People watch those for a reason. They want to feel warm and happy. It's why I read romance. Even though they sometimes break me along the way."

"You're going to have to tell me which books I need to read then."

Her brows rose. "You would read them?"

"Of course. I want to know what you like, Nessa." I hadn't quite meant to say that, but there was no taking it back now.

"Oh," she whispered. "Yes, I'll find a series for us to read together."

"Would you reread something, or would it be something new?"

"I don't know yet. I'll find something." She smiled, and I leaned forward and kissed her again. Her pencil dropped from her hand, and she groaned.

"You are so good at that."

"I try," I whispered and kissed her again.

She groaned once more, wrapping her arms around my neck. I deepened the kiss, then reached around and gripped her by the hips, picking her up. Her eyes widened as she pulled away slightly.

"How did you do that? You are so freaking strong."

"Just you wait," I winked and then leaned forward, biting her lip before I kissed away the sting. She wrapped her legs around my waist as I carried her to the bed. I gently set her on the mattress before I stripped her, ever so slowly. First her pants, then her top. She groaned as I lapped at and placed kisses along her body, trying to take in every inch of her, savor every breath. She lay naked before me as I stripped off my shirt and leaned down, bending myself between her legs as I looked my fill. Her pussy was wet, inviting. I lapped and licked, spreading her folds.

"You're so pretty. So wet."

"Only for you," she whispered.

"I'm going to have to do a better job, then," I said before licking and sucking more. I ate her out as she came, licking her clit as she rode my face. She came twice in an almost unending burst before I finally pulled away and flipped her onto her stomach. She groaned and pushed against me, but I reached out and smacked her on the ass. She shivered before pressing into my hold, and I slowly rubbed away the sting.

"You like?" I asked, being careful with her. Oh, so careful. I always would be. No matter what happened between us.

"I do," she whispered.

I spanked her again before reaching around and plucking at her nipples. I twisted harder than I had before, and she let out a shocked gasp. She froze, and I did the same.

"Too much?"

"No. I just…wow. I think I liked that."

"Good, then." I did the same to the other nipple, and she let out a shocked gasp before moaning. I slid my hand between her thighs, cupping her. I knew she was even wetter than she had been before. It seemed my little Nessa liked this. Good.

I rubbed my jean-clad cock against her heat before reaching around for the water bottle I had set near the bed earlier. I opened it, grateful for its insulated metal, and pulled out an ice cube. I rolled her onto her back, and she widened her eyes.

"What are you going to do with that?"

"You'll see." I gently rubbed the ice cube across her nipple, and she let out a shocked gasp, immediately putting her hands above her head. I nearly came at the sight; at how she submitted to me, even though that wasn't what we were doing. We didn't have that kind of relationship, and I wasn't ready for anything like that, but we were playing and being safe. That was all that mattered.

I slowly played with her nipples, using the ice and my warm mouth to send her over the edge again, but it wasn't until I slid the ice between her folds, and she bucked against my hand, that I knew she was mine. She came again, and then I stripped quickly as she shook, her entire body pink and flushed. I slid a condom over my cock, spread her thighs, and pistoned inside her.

She arched off the bed, and I latched onto her mouth, pinning her hips to the bed as I pounded into her. She groaned, scratching her nails down my back, and I knew I would treasure those marks for as long as they lasted. Hell, I would probably feel them far longer than they were ever in evidence. I couldn't breathe, couldn't do anything. All I wanted to do was have her forever. And because that couldn't happen, I pushed away those thoughts and kept going.

I was fucking happy. And Nessa was mine.

I followed her orgasm as she clamped down on my cock and did my best not to think about what would happen after the semester and the year were up. I kissed her again, rolled to the side, my back to the door, and just held her as we both came down.

Tanner walked in at that minute. "Are you fucking kidding me?" I shouted and then growled.

Nessa giggled and pushed herself against my body as I slowly wrapped a blanket around us both.

I glared over my shoulder at my roommate.

He had his hands over his eyes and was cursing. "Shit. You didn't notice that the power was out?"

I looked around. It was indeed dark. "Not really," I said, still balls-deep in Nessa.

"Well, fuck. The power's out. A storm's coming. Batten down the hatches, or I guess you're doing your own battening down. Not that it's a euphemism, but I'm going to make it work. Fuck. I didn't see anything of you, Nessa, but I've seen way too much of my roommate now."

Tanner slammed the door on his way out, and I looked down at Nessa before we both laughed.

"Well, then," Nessa said, blinking up at me. "I don't know if I can be embarrassed anymore."

"Ah, well, I'll probably feel this later." I leaned down and kissed her. "We should probably make sure everything's okay."

"Maybe. Or perhaps we can just stay under the blankets and forget the rest of the world."

And as much as I wanted to do that, as much as I

knew she wanted to do that, we both got up after a moment. Still, I held her close.

I was fucking falling for her, and I knew it was a damn mistake.

After all, Nessa wasn't for me.

Fifteen

Nessa

I shelved another book and smiled at a customer, my head aching. I hadn't slept the night before, homework taking a toll. It was my fault. I'd gotten lost in my book and had written three chapters back-to-back, putting out as much of my grief and frustration as I could. My heroine might not be on the same journey, as she was dealing with the fae and dragons, but I had personal dragons to slay. Not that I was sure I could eradicate them. But perhaps I could try. Or I could at least organize those dragons and fae into little boxes so I could find my path. Either way, I had worked on my book when I probably shouldn't have and had gotten behind on my homework. That meant little sleep before this morning. I didn't have classes today, only a full shift and then a girls' night at the house. We didn't get to have them as often anymore, and even then, Mackenzie was new to them.

At our old house, before we had lost Corinne, we'd had full-fledged girls' nights at least twice a month where we had a theme, awesome food, and just hung out together as we talked about boys and life and classes. Discussed movies that we wanted to watch. We sometimes even made it to the living room to watch some. We simply enjoyed one another. All of that female bonding and life was everything. Corinne had been a huge part of that. She had been the first to suggest it and had pushed us to do it more often. And then she died, and everything had changed. Although, that wasn't the only reason.

Mackenzie and Elise were spending more and more time at the guys' house, their relationships with Pacey and Dillon getting more serious with each passing day. I had a feeling one or both of them would end up engaged by the time we graduated. I didn't see a problem with that as my parents had gotten involved during college. Planning your future with someone that you loved while making sure you met your goals and plans at the same time was something worthwhile.

Difficult, but practical. I wasn't doing that. I ignored the slight twinge I felt in my heart. I focused on the connections I had while trying to make plans for a future I wasn't sure about. Miles wouldn't be in that future. That much I knew.

"You're thinking hard again," Everly said as she walked towards me.

I looked over at her then and smiled. "My brain can't quit sometimes."

"No worries. You were thinking hard enough that you missed the fact that your shift ended ten minutes ago." I looked down at my phone and blinked. "Oh. I didn't even realize."

"You didn't. But now you can go and spend some time with the girls and eat pizza or whatever you guys do to enjoy yourselves."

"Mackenzie and Natalie are craving butter chicken and vindaloo."

"Really?" Everly asked, her eyes wide.

"Yes, we have a few recipes, and our neighbors gave us some spices since they know what they're doing while we're still learning."

"I'm jealous."

"If we have any leftovers the guys don't get to first, I'll bring you some."

My boss smiled at me. "That sounds like a plan. Or

I guess you can just come over and cook it at our house someday."

"I didn't say I was the one cooking tonight," I said with a laugh, shaking my head.

"True, true. Have fun. I will see you on Monday."

"Sounds good, thank you." I kissed her cheek and grabbed my stuff to head out.

It was nice having Everly around because I missed my mom. I knew she couldn't be my mom age-wise, but she just had this presence that soothed like my mom used to have. I missed her so damn much. She had been everything to me. Some days, I still couldn't believe she was gone. It felt like just yesterday she had been reading the first draft of my book and smiling, not necessarily pushing me but being my support system and my pillar for pursuing a career as an author and an English professor. I didn't have any lofty dreams of getting a seven-figure contract right out of the gate with a movie deal and an astronomical print run. No, I didn't think that would ever happen to me. And while it would be wonderful and would help my bills and the medical bills that came from Mom, it wasn't reality. I just wanted to see my book on bookshelves. That *was* something on my path. I also wanted to learn and create and watch others do the same. Maybe it wouldn't be a job that made me millions, but it could hopefully create a life for me.

At least, that's what I hoped.

I pulled into the gas station near the exit off the highway and got out to fill my tank. The hairs on the back of my neck prickled, and I frowned and looked over my shoulder. Nobody was there, just a few people either filling up or walking into the convenience store. I frowned and shook my head. I was just tired and feeling things. Yet why did it feel like somebody's eyes were on me? Not that it could happen. Someone's gaze, not their eyeballs. I groaned at my weird editor joke and quickly finished filling up my gas tank. I pulled into the driveway, got out, and grabbed my things before heading in. The house smelled of spices, warmth, and bread. My stomach grumbled, and the girls looked over at me from the kitchen. "You're here. We haven't burned anything yet," Mackenzie said.

Elise shushed her. "You know better than to jinx us."

Natalie laughed. "We already had to call the neighbor. When they didn't pick up right away, we called Aiden."

"Aiden helped?" I asked.

"Yes, because we have a recipe, but we wanted to make sure. He helped us through the beginning parts. The neighbor's recipe was very detailed, and when they called back, everything was great."

"I'm glad we haven't burned down the house yet."

I cringed. "Okay, should I go outside and spin in a circle or something?"

"No, but here's some salt," Natalie said, her expression serious. "Seriously, throw it over your shoulder."

"The whole shaker?"

She sighed. "Nessa, you know the rules."

"I do," I said as I sprinkled some salt onto my palm and tossed it over my shoulder.

"Better now?" I asked.

"Marginally. We may have to go out there and dance naked later."

"I didn't say I was dancing naked," I said with a laugh.

"That will get the neighbors talking for sure," Elise said as she handed over a drink. "We're just doing champagne tonight. Is that okay?"

"That sounds amazing." I reached and took the glass from her.

"We haven't started yet. It's our first glass." Mackenzie held up hers. We clinked glasses and grinned.

"To girls' night," Natalie said, beaming.

"To girls' night," I whispered before taking a sip. The bubbles burst on my tongue, playing down my throat as I swallowed. "This is good stuff."

"It's one of Dillon's brother's favorites. Not the

expensive bougie kind, but one we can afford," Elise said on a laugh.

"Yes, because I'm poor. Remember?" I said with a wince.

The girls all knew my financial troubles, and while I never hid them from them, it still felt weird. I knew Natalie and even Elise came from families with far more money than mine had. Mackenzie did, as well, but she was more on my family's level.

Natalie, though? Natalie was out of this world in the circles her family lived in. Yet, she was still our Natalie. One of my best friends.

"Okay, let's go over what we have tonight," Mackenzie said as she set down her glass, clapping her hands in front of her. "We have way too much food, but that's good because you know the guys will probably end up wanting to eat us out of house and home later if they stop by."

Natalie's head shot up. "I thought it was girls' night. Guys don't come to girls' night," she said and then winced. "Wow, don't I sound like the sad little lonely virgin left at the table?" she said dramatically, putting her hand on her forehead.

I crossed my eyes. "Oh, stop." I looked at Mackenzie. "They're not coming, are they?"

"They were told they weren't invited," Elise said primly. "However, we know them. Right?"

I sighed. "I told Miles it was girls' night. He'll probably actually listen to me," I said.

"Miles is the good one," Natalie grumbled. "I bet you Tanner will be the one to push them all here."

I met Mackenzie's and Elise's gazes. But, once again, we didn't touch that. I had no idea what was wrong with her and Tanner. But it seemed they seriously did not like each other.

"If anything, we know Pacey's the one who puts them all together," Mackenzie said, and I nodded. "Pretty much."

She smiled, and I returned it. We were good now. Especially now that I was with Miles. Things weren't strained when it came to Pacey and me. Yes, I had been an idiot, but we were all over it, and Mackenzie and Pacey were just so freaking cute that it didn't matter anymore what feelings I thought I once had for him.

"Anyway," Elise said, "they may show up for food later. But they're not allowed to stay. I promise. This is girls' night. We talk about guys. We don't let them inside the house."

"So, we'll shove to-go boxes at them through a crack in the door. Maybe throw it at them."

"Oh, good, then we can clean up the mess later because it's not like any of us have any aim."

"I have aim," Natalie said. "I was captain of my softball team, thank you very much."

"Then we can go to the emergency room because you're going to beat Tanner to submission," I said with a laugh.

Natalie's cheeks pinked. "I didn't hurt him. Much. I mean, I can't get in trouble and go to jail for hurting him. I have priorities."

"That is true," Mackenzie said. "Okay, now chop-chop, let's get everything into the living room. Nessa, you're wearing far too many clothes. Go get in your pajamas and take that bra off."

"I feel like the guys all just groaned somewhere hearing that," I said dryly, and Elise grinned.

"The guys might be expecting teddies and pillow fights, but they're going to end up getting pajamas with holes in them, no bras, and facials." She coughed. "I mean, you know, the face stuff. The creams and stuff." She kept stuttering and rambling, and we all started laughing. "I mean actual face creams and firming serums. Oh my God, why does everything facial-related that *isn't* sex-related sound like it's about dicks?"

I laughed so hard my side ached as I made my way to my bedroom, champagne in hand. I took another sip, feeling far happier than I had in a while. No, that wasn't true. Miles made me happy. And as if I had conjured him out of thin air, my phone buzzed, and I looked down.

Miles: *I'll keep the guys away as long as I can, but they know there's good food there, and I know you're making a lot. We may be there in about an hour. I'm sorry, babe.*

I grinned, humming a bit and a little warm from the champagne and just seeing his name.

Me: *I'm sure I can let you in through the window. You need to be quiet.*

Miles: *Babe, we both know that you're the one who's never quiet.*

I blushed and pressed my thighs together. Damn, that man.

Me: *Okay, fine. I guess you can gag me.*

Miles: *Damn it, now I have a hard-on in the kitchen, and the guys are staring at me.*

Me: *You're the one who started it. I guess I'll see you soon. Make sure Tanner doesn't annoy Natalie.*

Miles: *I don't know what's up between the two of them, but I'll make sure he doesn't annoy her. And, frankly, he has to work tonight, so I don't even think he'd show.*

I winced, even though he couldn't see me.

Me: *That will make things weird if it's the three of us couples and Natalie is by herself.*

Miles: *Shit. We won't come inside. If we even show up at all. I'll convince the guys or something.*

I sighed, frowning as I quickly stripped off my clothes and put on my pajamas.

Me: *No, I want to see your face. Which is probably a mistake. But yes I want to see you.*

Miles: *That makes me happy to hear. We'll figure something out. And we won't make Natalie feel bad. I promise.*

Me: *Good. I'll see you soon.*

Miles: *Not soon enough.*

I bit my lip as I set my phone down and shook my head. I was getting in far too deep, too quickly, when it came to Miles, but that was fine. I'd work things out. I would find a way to pay for the next semester, even if working two jobs killed me. But I would not lose this feeling. This sense of happiness that I had had nothing to do with champagne. Though I knew it couldn't only be about Miles. At least, that's what I kept telling myself.

Sixteen

Miles

I had Nessa's legs around my shoulders and her sweet pussy on my face. I needed nothing more in the world. I groaned as I licked and sucked, spreading her folds with my fingers as I delved my tongue deep inside her.

My hips worked as we lay on our sides, my cock sliding between Nessa's lips gently as she licked at me. We were in my bed, the two of us taking our time pleasuring one another before classes.

We'd barely had time to see each other over the past week between school and work, but we were stealing this time for ourselves. And having Nessa's pussy on my face was the best way to enjoy that time.

"Miles," she moaned as I touched her *just* right.

I grinned, then went back to my breakfast, taking my fill until, finally, she came, her body bowing as her mouth tightened on my dick. The dueling sensations sent shivers over my body, and I came, stilling my hips so I wouldn't pound into her mouth like my body wanted to.

I gently petted her thighs, bringing her down off her high as I did the same, and when she groaned again, leaning her head on my inner thigh, I moved so I sat, and she could lay on my lap as I ran my hands all over her body.

"That's one way to wake up," she whispered, looking up at me, her body warm, her nipples hard, her skin pink and dewy. I gently cupped her breasts, running my thumb across her nipple before leaning down to kiss her. She looked up at me and grinned.

"Hi," she whispered.

"Hi. I know you have to go to class, but I'm glad you stayed the night. This was the best way to wake up."

She smiled, even though her eyes looked slightly bashful. Spending the night was a big deal, something we hadn't done before. Ensuring each other that we weren't taking too big of a step or deluding ourselves that this could only be for a night was a tricky balancing act. At least, that's what I told myself as I slowly ran my hands down her body again.

"I hate that I have to get to class soon."

"You can shower and get ready here," I whispered.

"I do need to at least shower because I don't need to be smelling like sex as I'm sitting in the middle of statistics." My cock hardened at her words, and considering that she was lying on my lap, she laughed.

"There is no time for more of that, mister."

"I can't help it. I feel like we should make time."

I trailed my fingers down to cup her between the legs, and she arched into me.

"Miles," she warned, and I grinned.

"I'm sorry," I said, not sorry in the slightest.

"I'm going to use your shower, and then I'm heading to class. So, you'd better stop fingering me or we'll never leave."

I had two fingers deep inside her as she arched, and I flicked my thumb over her clit, gently bringing her to another release that surprised us both.

She blinked up at me, her mouth parted. "Well, then, it seems that all that studying has led to amazing things."

"I try my best." I patted her hip, then helped her sit up before kissing her again. "I'm meeting with my brother today, and then I have to do a few things around the house and grade some papers. Will I see you later?"

I didn't like the need in my voice because I wasn't sure what answer I wanted. If I saw Nessa later, did that mean it meant something? Or were we counting down the days until we left each other?

What was wrong with me? Why couldn't I just take things one day at a time? Instead, I had to keep twisting it in my head to us leaving each other rather than us spending time with one another now.

There was indeed something wrong with me. I needed to take a step back and breathe. Only I didn't think that was going to happen. Not when it came to Nessa.

"I'm not sure," she said, hedging. I understood.

While I was falling in love with her, she did her best not to fall into anything with me. While I understood it, it didn't make it any easier. I kissed her again and then helped her get out of bed so she could shower. I did my best not to think about her in there. All naked and wet and ready for me. She had to go to school. And I needed some distance.

If I weren't careful, I wouldn't want to let her go.

The first rule of our relationship was that we needed to let each other go.

Even if it broke me in the end.

She left soon after, kissing me goodbye, and I was

grateful that I didn't see any of the roommates as I walked her out. I didn't need their questioning glances or, worse, their pitying ones. While Pacey and Dillon were in serious relationships that I knew could and would last forever, everybody knew mine wasn't. This was only supposed to be a fling, a time between friends.

It wasn't for me, though, and that was something I would have to deal with.

I quickly showered, cleaning up after the long evening and just trying to push out thoughts of Nessa. We had only started our relationship. I couldn't be in anything more than like with her.

I needed to focus on grading, homework, and my brother. He had a teacher workday and planned to spend a couple of hours with me before my parents got off work. Mom was only working a half-day, so I was babysitting the kid who didn't need supervision every hour of every day. I wasn't going to say that because it wasn't my place anymore. Aaron was my brother, not my kid. I had already shown them that I wasn't good at making choices when it came to keeping my siblings safe—at least according to them and my nightmares. I didn't need to break down and hurt Aaron in the process.

I made my way downstairs, got myself a cup of coffee, and pulled out a bagel with some cream cheese. Dillon and Pacey were already gone, and Tanner was probably still sleeping. I knew he worked late and needed as much sleep as possible. He worked even longer hours than Nessa did, and I wasn't sure how he kept up with his classes and workload.

I shook my head and then looked down at my phone as the motion sensor alerted that someone was out there. Aaron waved at the camera, and I grinned, stuck half a bagel in my mouth, and made my way to the front door. I opened it. Aaron smiled and stole the bagel from me, eating the rest of it in three bites. I shook my head, my lips twitching. "That was mine."

"You were too slow. Got any more?"

"I do. Come on."

"Mom said I had to do my homework."

"You do. I have some grading and homework, as well. Did Mom and Dad not come in to drop you off?" I asked him while frowning.

"Mom is probably still watching us." He waved over his shoulder, and I looked up and indeed saw my mom's car there, she flashed her lights and then drove off. I shook my head.

"Okay, time for babysitting."

"I'm not a baby."

I grinned at the affront in his voice and headed to the kitchen. I pulled out two more bagels and toasted them as I made hot cocoa for the kid.

"I like coffee, too."

"I'm not giving you coffee. I'm not dealing with the wrath of Mom and Dad."

"We all know that wrath is interesting," he grumbled, and I gave him a look.

"What's wrong?" I asked.

"Nothing. Just normal parent stuff."

"Normal *parent stuff* that gets you all grumbly?"

I handed over the hot cocoa and proceeded to spread cream cheese over both bagels. I plated one of them for him and the other for me and gave him a look. "Spill the beans, kid."

"They're just stressing out because they know you're leaving, and that means they're tightening the strings on me. I'm not even allowed to join soccer next year because of all the away games."

I set my coffee on the island, my eyes wide. "What?" Shock slammed into me. Aaron was a legitimately fantastic soccer player. He played club ball and for the school team. I knew that if he kept at it, he could likely get a scholarship. Maybe not go pro unless he wanted to, but he had choices. I had always been semi-athletic, but academic classes had been more interesting to me, so I had only played soccer for a couple of years. It wasn't my thing. For Aaron? It was his life.

"How is that okay?" I asked.

"It's not. They're saying no. That I'm spending too

much time on it and not on school. And, honestly, because I'm not there with them enough. The travel schedule for next year is double what it is now. And while I realize it would take a lot of time and effort on Mom's and Dad's parts, they're more worried about me not being at their beck and call. Or at least under their thumbs."

I frowned. "What the hell? I can talk to them."

He shook his head, and I knew what he was going to say next. "It would only make it worse."

And that was the truth. Me standing up for my brother would indeed only make it worse. How the hell had it gotten this way? I hated it.

"You're going to be gone next year. Off at grad school like you should be, which means I'm not going to be able to see you. Unless you come back for the holidays."

"Maybe I can find a way to stay. There are enough universities in Colorado that if I stay, I can do my grad school thing here and still be able to help out." Part of me wanted to stay in the state anyway. I had friends here.

"Would you be hurting your dream in the process?"

I frowned. "I don't know. CU has a good program. And stipends. It was on my list anyway." Not at the top of it because I had wanted to move, but my brother needed me. And, fuck, Nessa would be here, too. Not that I could let her be the central part of my decisions.

Still, there had to be something I could do.

"I don't want to talk about it anymore," Aaron said, picking at his bagel.

I nodded. "No problem. Let's talk about classes."

"Or we can just play games," he said, grinning.

"No, I have work to do. Therefore, you have work to do." The doorbell rang again, and I frowned, looking down at the motion sensor.

My stomach tightened, and I held back a curse.

"What's wrong?" Aaron asked.

"Mom is back," I growled.

Aaron gave me a sad look. "Glad I didn't unpack," he grumbled.

"I guess not," I whispered and headed to the door.

Mom raised her chin, even though she had a smile on her face. "It turns out I have the day off, so you don't need to stick with Aaron. I'll take him home."

"We're good here."

"I'm sure you are. But you know, just in case."

She didn't need to finish that statement. *Just in case.* Just in case I got drunk and behind the wheel. Just in case I killed my baby brother like I had killed my twin. I knew what she meant.

I looked at my mother then, and I didn't see a

single lick of trust in her eyes. She didn't trust me with him.

If I stayed in Colorado, if I fought for Aaron to stay in soccer and do what he loved, she would continue not trusting me. Maybe that would be worth it, though. Aaron needed an advocate. And, somehow, my parents weren't that.

Aaron stood behind me, his bag over his shoulder. "Okay. Bye, Miles."

He wasn't even fighting it anymore. Then again, was I?

"Did you have hot chocolate? What's on your lip?" Mom asked, her eyes narrowed.

"Yes, he had hot chocolate. And I had coffee. I didn't let him have coffee. How's that?" I asked, my tone grating.

My mom narrowed her eyes. "You don't have to speak to me that way."

"Just go." I sighed.

"Miles..." Aaron began.

"I'll see you soon."

"We'll see," my mom shot back, and my eyes widened.

"No, I'll see him soon. And we're going to have a talk."

"Excuse me?" my mom said, and it felt off. They had been so overprotective of me for so long. But now, they seemed to have switched their focus to Aaron. Which meant I was the one being pushed out. What the hell had happened?

"Bye, Mom," I whispered and looked at Aaron. "Goodbye. I'll talk to you soon."

"Okay," Aaron said, his shoulders hunched.

Mom gave me a look but headed down the front steps, Aaron in tow.

I needed to fix this. Somehow, I needed to fix this. It wasn't going to happen standing on my porch when I didn't have a plan in place.

I closed the door, leaned my head against the wood, and groaned.

"Do you want to talk about it?"

I whirled and looked at Tanner, who had my cup of coffee in his hand, sipping.

"Why does everyone keep stealing shit from me?"

"I'd say it's because you let it happen, but I'm not going to kick a puppy right now."

"I'm not a fucking puppy," I growled.

"No, you're not. I'm serious if you want to talk."

"They don't fucking trust me."

"Did you do something to cause that?"

I looked at him then and realized he didn't know. "It's a long story."

"I've got time."

I sighed and told him the tragic story of Rachelle. I

didn't go into too much detail, not as much as I had with Nessa because I wasn't sure I could, but I told him as much as I was able.

Tanner's eyes widened for a fraction of a second, and he set down my coffee. "Fuck. I'm sorry."

My gut churned. "Me, too. I can't bring her back. It seems all I can do is make my parents not trust me over and over again."

"You need to talk to them about it."

"They're not going to listen."

"For Aaron's sake—and yours—you need to try."

"I know," I whispered. "I think I'm going to have to stay in Colorado, though. Try to get into CU. I'm working on applications now. It was always on the list, but now I need to make it a priority."

"And that would make you closer to Nessa," he said.

I looked up at him then and shook my head. "All the mistakes I've made? Everything on Nessa's shoulders? She's going to need someone who can actually be there for her. Someone who's enough. Do you think I'm that guy?" I hadn't even realized I'd said the words until they were out of my mouth. I wanted to take them back.

Tanner looked at me then and shook his head. My stomach fell, but then he spoke. "Sometimes, you're more than you think you are, Miles. Remember that.

You're a good guy. You don't need to figure everything out right now. You can take your time. And we're here for you. Now, I'm taking your coffee and going back to my room to work. You should go work, too."

I growled and took my coffee back. "Make your own."

Tanner grinned and winked. "That's a start. That's a start."

Then my roommate walked off, and I shook my head, wondering why the hell everyone was testing me today.

And what the hell I was going to do about it.

Seventeen

Nessa

I smiled up at the sky as I lifted my face to the sun, closing my eyes. It felt so good to breathe, to be out in the outside world and know what the weather was without having to look it up on my phone. I had been sequestered in my room on campus and at work for what seemed like forever, trying to get caught up. I was working as many hours as Everly could provide to me, and I still wasn't sure it would be enough to pay whatever my loans and stipends and scholarships didn't cover for the rest of the following semester. I didn't want to take Dad's money when I knew he needed it more.

Tuition would be calling any day now, and as I looked at the mail in my hand, I knew it was coming up quickly. My final installment was due; I saw the red words on the envelope in my hand. And I knew that if I weren't careful, they wouldn't let me back. This last semester might be for nothing because I still had one little payment left that wasn't so tiny. I'd kept telling myself that I would be fine for a few more months, but now those months had run out. Being on a payment plan meant I needed to *plan*, and though I had, it still didn't seem to be enough.

I groaned, annoyed with myself for ruining this slice of warmth I had let myself have. We were nearing winter, fall having come and gone out of nowhere. And Colorado winters meant four seasons per day sometimes, and below-freezing wasn't out of bounds.

Still, right now, it was warm on my face, and I needed to remember that and soak it in. There was light in the darkness, a way out of the cold.

I let out a breath and went through the rest of the mail, organizing it by person and household issues. I stepped inside, set my keys on the entryway table, and put each set of mail into piles. The final piece had me frowning as I picked up the letter postmarked for the city, with Miles' name in the corner. I frowned and opened it, a smile slowly sliding onto my face.

Thinking of you. Just wanted you to know I believe in you.

I grinned and set the note down on the table. I couldn't believe he'd wasted a stamp on that, but it made me smile, so maybe it wasn't a waste, after all. I shook my head, clutched the letter to my chest, and went back to my room, setting it down with my other things. I also had the bill in my hand and tried not to think about that too hard. I had to open it.

I swallowed hard, wondering if it was too early to have a drink, and opened up the letter. I nearly dropped it, my hands shaking.

I knew how much I owed, but there were fees and taxes there that hadn't been before. Or maybe I had missed them. I didn't know. But, dear God, with the added medical insurance that came with school, I wasn't sure I would be able to afford to do anything. And I needed medical insurance. I had medicine that I took daily. I had asthma and needed my inhaler. Yet I couldn't breathe just then.

I wouldn't be able to afford next semester. There was no way unless Dad sold the house immediately or I won the lottery.

I couldn't afford this final payment. And if I didn't ask my dad, who I knew wouldn't be able to help, not with Mom's medical bills chomping at his heels, I would have to drop out.

I couldn't pay for my last semester, and I wouldn't be able to pay for even this final bill.

Tears formed at the backs of my eyes, and I swallowed hard, my hands shaking.

The doorbell rang, and I frowned, wondering who it could be. I picked up Miles' letter along with the bill, needing something to negate the negativity. Sadly, I wasn't sure even that would work.

I opened the door, and Miles stood there. All I wanted to do was lean on him, hold onto him and have him tell me that everything would be okay.

That was a mistake, though, and I couldn't let that happen. I needed to be strong without relying on him. He would be gone soon, and the more I relied on him, the worse it would hurt—just like with Pacey. I might not have loved him like I thought I had, but I *had* relied on him as emotional support. Something that had slapped back at me when I realized I had been mistaken about my feelings.

It had hurt when I had to walk away, realizing that I had made a mistake.

This would hurt far more.

"What's wrong?" Miles asked as he walked into the house.

He cupped my face, and I wanted to lean into his

touch. Instead, I pulled away and saw the hurt in his expression, but I had to ignore it.

I couldn't let myself get hurt again. And I couldn't hurt him by delaying the inevitable.

"I'm fine." I looked down at the note, my heart breaking even as my voice shook. "Thank you for the letter."

He gave me an odd look. "Letter?"

Foreboding slid up my spine, and I looked at him, meeting his gaze. His eyes broke me, the way they saw too much. Yet I couldn't let him see any more. "The one you wrote me. It was like the text you sent."

"I don't know what you're talking about, Nessa."

I looked at him then and held out the letter. He didn't grab it. Instead, he read it as I held it. He cursed, a scowl etching his face.

"We're calling that detective."

"What?" I asked, licking my suddenly dry lips. "What do you mean? This isn't from you?" I already assumed that, of course, but I needed to hear the words. I needed him to tell me this was a mistake. I couldn't take any more than I'd already been given.

"Nessa, I've never given you flowers. I should have, but every time I thought about it, it creeped me out and made me think of Xander. And that letter? I didn't write it. It's not my handwriting."

"It isn't?" I looked down at it, and then it dawned

on me. It wasn't. These lines were slanted just a little differently. I had seen his handwriting numerous times as we went over homework, and yet I hadn't noticed. I had been wrong.

"I shouldn't have held this. Don't they need it for evidence or something? Oh my God, why is he doing this, Miles?"

He scowled and walked to the kitchen, leaving me behind as I stood there, my heart racing. I swallowed hard. "Miles," I said.

"I'm getting a plastic bag, and we're going to call the cops."

"My fingerprints are all over it. And I don't know if those cop shows are actually right. I know nothing about forensic evidence."

"Neither do I, but this will be as good as it gets." He held out the bag, and I slid the envelope and letter into it, my hands shaking.

"Why is this happening?"

"I don't know, but we're going to call the detective."

"Okay, I can do that."

"We can do that."

Again, it reminded me that I needed to stop this. I had to do this on my own. I couldn't focus on every detail and remain composed. Which meant, I had to do something that would hurt, even if this might not be the right time. Hell, maybe this was the *best* time.

"I will. I'll call him. I'll figure it out. But first, I need to say a few things." Why did my voice sound so cool? Why did it feel as if I'd already fallen and there was no hope for survival?

"No, first, you're going to call the detective."

"I just...I need you to listen to me," I said, trying to push all thoughts of everything else in my life out of the way.

Those hurt, and if I focused on them, I wouldn't make it. I would sit down and curl into a ball, and I wouldn't fight back. And that was not the Nessa I thought I was. I thought I was a person who could fight back and take care of herself. I pushed my friends to fight for themselves, yet here I was, relying on everybody else and wanting to run away from my problems. I wasn't going to do that. I would handle this now before Miles got hurt any more. Before I lost everything. Before *he* lost everything.

Then I would deal with the reality of my situation and burst the fantasy bubble of whatever this was and could be.

"I don't think I can do this," I said quickly.

He looked at me then, confusion on his face. "I'll call the detective. You don't have to worry. I'm here for you, Nessa."

Shattered. Broken. There would be nothing left after this. "No, not that. I will handle that. I will handle it all, just like I always have."

"What the hell are you talking about, Nessa?" he asked, his voice slightly growly.

"I don't think I can do this, Miles." I gestured between us. "This is too fast and too much. I know I'm going to be a horrible person, and everyone's going to hate me for this, but you're leaving anyway. And I don't even know if I can stay for the whole year. Even though we thought I could, I'm not sure I can. And I can't talk about it right now, but this is just too much. *You're going to leave anyway, Miles.* I don't want either of us getting hurt more than we already are. So, you should go. I'll handle this. I promise."

I wasn't even sure what I was saying at that point. I needed Miles gone. If he stayed, I'd break beyond redemption.

I couldn't let myself fall deeper or shatter into a thousand pieces when he left me. I had to be the one to let him go.

He blinked at me, the bewilderment in his eyes a tear across my heart. "What the hell, Nessa? No, this isn't how you react to this. We're going to handle it together."

"There is no *us* and *together*, Miles." And as soon as I said the words, I knew if I didn't push him away, he would stay. That was the guy Miles was. He was someone who would always remain. Who would be there because he hadn't been able to be there for the one person who mattered the most. He would always take care of everyone else.

I couldn't let him drain himself of everything he had left to protect me, when he'd leave us both broken in the end.

"You need to go. Just let me handle this. We can go back to being friends. Or you can never speak to me again because I'm such a bitch. But you can't stay. I can't do this right now with you. Don't you understand that? I need you to go."

"Nessa," he whispered.

Tears threatened, but I pushed them back. It was the only way. "Please. I can't do this. I can't deal with school and you and whatever the hell Xander wants. So leave. I'll lock the doors. I'll call the detective. I'll even call the girls. I don't know. You can't be here."

"Meaning you can rely on everyone *but* me." His voice was ice, and I hated myself, but I would hurt him more if he stayed. I knew that. It was what I did. He needed to leave.

I needed him to go.

"Please, Miles."

"I'm calling the girls," he said, his voice hollow. "We're going to talk about this."

"There's nothing to talk about, Miles," I lied. I was such a liar. "I can't think with you around."

He looked like I'd hit him, his whole body jerking at the blow. I hated myself.

"Okay, then. If that's what you want. I always told you it was your call. Always. I'm still calling the girls. Lock the door. Call the fucking detective. Xander's out there somewhere. He's fucking stalking you. And you know what? I'm going to give you some time, but this isn't over. You and me? We have a lot to talk about, and I know this is probably too much for you, so I'll go, I'll give you that space. But not forever, Nessa. We're going to talk."

"There's nothing to talk about," I lied again, and he shook his head and leaned forward.

"There's everything to talk about. You're asking me to go, so I will. You asked Xander to go, and he didn't. That's the only reason I'm leaving." And on that parting note, he left. I locked the door behind him, pulling out my phone as I slowly slid to the floor, tears falling down my cheeks.

I needed to call the detective. I needed to reach the bursar. I needed to talk to my father. I needed to do everything except cry, ending up in a puddle as I broke.

With every step Miles took away from me, I regretted it. He was gone. I had pushed him out. He'd said he would come back to fight, but was I worth fighting for?

I was nothing. I was only a burden.

He walked away because I told him to. He hadn't wanted to push himself on me. That was the type of man Miles was.

That was the type of man I had hurt. The kind I had pushed away.

The type I didn't want to push away.

Eighteen

Miles

"You're going to head over soon?" Dillon asked, and I looked up from my coffee, pulling myself out of my mind.

"I'll be there soon."

"What's going on? Are you okay?" my roommate asked.

I shrugged. "I'm fine. Just a long night."

A long night where I hadn't slept because all I had wanted to do was head back over to the girls' house and talk to Nessa to try and make her understand that I was fucking in love with her. That wouldn't have done anything, though. As soon as I'd left, I had called the girls, and they had run over. Dillon and Pacey had, as well. All of them had been there for Nessa, and they had given me weird and accusatory looks when I said that I needed to deal with my work. It had been a lie, and they all knew it. Nobody understood why I had left her alone. I hadn't left her alone, though. Not really. I had sat out in the car until the others showed up, and then I had driven away. Despite what she wanted, I hadn't left her. That might not have been her exact wishes, but I wasn't about to leave her alone where Xander could come out of nowhere. He had hurt her once. He wasn't going to fucking do it again.

I knew she was scared. I knew she was overwhelmed. And I was the easiest person to knock out of her life. I would give her a moment to think. To breathe. And then we would talk. I was in love with her, and I had to find a way to make what we had before she pushed me away work. I didn't want this to be temporary. Only I had a feeling it might need to be. If there was too much in her life, things she couldn't handle, she would push out the one thing she could. Me.

I hated everything right now.

Life. The circumstances. Myself.

Never Nessa, though. I couldn't.

"You're looking sad again. Do you want to tell me

what happened between you and Nessa?" Dillon asked. I looked up at him, unaware that I'd been standing and looking out into the distance.

"I'm fine. And nothing's going on with Nessa and me," I lied.

"Liar," he said, shaking his head. "You guys helped me before with Elise. I can help you."

I shook my head. "I don't need help. I need to think."

"Something happened before we got there. You wouldn't have left her otherwise."

"I didn't necessarily *leave* her. I don't want to talk about it, okay?"

"Okay, but we're here if you need us. And Nessa's not going to be left alone. None of the girls are. Pacey and I are taking turns sleeping there."

"Good," I said, relief and a bit of jealousy seeping through.

Dillon leaned forward. "If you want to be there, all you have to do is tell me. I'll give you space."

I shook my head. "No, I don't need to be there. I don't think she wants me there."

Dillon sighed. "I'm sorry."

"I'm sorry, too, but we'll figure it out. First, though, we have Pacey and Mackenzie's event."

They had won an award for the semester on one of their projects. The prize wasn't only dinner in their honor, it also meant that any grad school would fight for them now.

I was fucking happy for them, even if I wished there was a way for Nessa's major to have something similar. There were no English or writing scholarships for the final semester. Not the way there were for the sciences. While I appreciated the sciences—hell, it was my livelihood and future—I hated the idea that I couldn't do anything for Nessa. Again.

"We'll meet you there. Just don't be late, okay?"

I lifted my chin. "You know I hate being late."

"I do. I also know you're having a shit day."

An understatement. "I am, but it's what I do. I'll see you guys soon. I need to pick up a couple of things, grade a few papers, and then I'll be ready."

"Okay, good. See you then."

Dillon left, leaving me alone in the house. Pacey was already there as it was his event with Mackenzie, and Tanner had a seminar that morning and would head over soon.

I'd go later, unable to even bring my brother as I had planned. It was Saturday, so he didn't have school or soccer thanks to my parents pulling him out last week, but they weren't letting me take him anyway. I would have to deal with that later. Just not today. There wasn't enough time. Being typical *me*, I had made notes about what I wanted to say because, no matter what, I wouldn't leave my brother's life. I hadn't done anything wrong, something Mom and Dad needed to realize. I wasn't a bad person.

I refused to let them cut me out of my brother's life. Refused. I just needed to make a plan for my parents to understand that. No amount of me changing the person I had been before the accident had worked so far. I needed to find a different way, even if it hurt in the process.

I pulled on my suit jacket, not bothering with a tie. Mackenzie had said that I didn't need one, and I was grateful. I hated them. I cleaned off my glasses and sighed, figuring I should probably put in my contacts. It was cold out, and I hated when my glasses fogged up. I headed back upstairs to the bathroom, put in my contacts, and frowned as I looked at my phone. I saw Natalie's name. I wasn't sure Natalie had ever called me before. She had texted, but I didn't think I had ever heard her voice over the phone.

Anxiety filled me because she was supposed to be with Nessa. Wasn't she? Shit.

I picked up. "Natalie?"

"Oh, good, you answered. Can you pick up Nessa? Her car died."

"Why aren't you with her?" I asked as I stuffed my keys into my pocket and headed downstairs toward the door.

"I had to meet with my parents this morning, even though I wasn't planning on it. Elise was with Nessa, but she met up with Dillon. I think our wires got crossed. So, unfortunately, she's alone. She's fine, but her car won't start."

I cursed and stomped out to my vehicle. "She wasn't supposed to be alone," I growled.

"I know. I'm sorry. I thought she would have called you to come and pick her up. I am sorry. Please. She's safe, but she needs a ride."

"I've got it."

"I was surprised she didn't call you herself."

"Stop fishing, Natalie. I mean, I like you and all, but I'm not in the mood to deal."

"Fine. And thank you. Nessa's in the house, locked up tight, and won't answer the door for anyone but you. At least once I text her to say that you're on the way."

I cursed as I started the engine. "Oh, good. She'll feel great about that," I muttered.

"I can head over there and pick her up, I guess. It's just I'm halfway between the convention center and the house. I thought it would be easier for you, you know since you guys are dating and all."

"I've got it, Natalie," I gritted out. "Thank you."

"No, thank you. I am sorry. And I'm here if you need me."

"I know, Natalie. Drive safely and be safe. Did the cops say anything about where Xander was?" I asked.

"Nessa didn't tell you?"

"No," I said, my tone grating.

"Xander's in jail for a DUI," she said softly. "So, he can't get to her. Which is why our wires probably got crossed today. She's fine."

"Fine," I whispered, repeating her word.

"As fine as she can be with her heart broken, though from the sound of your voice, I have a feeling she might have done that herself. I'm not going to pry. Any more than I already am."

"Thank you, Natalie," I whispered.

"You're welcome. Now, fix things. You guys can fix things, right?"

"I shouldn't be on the phone while driving," I said, even though I was on my Bluetooth.

"Okay, I'm prying. Goodbye. Be safe."

"Goodbye," I muttered and hung up. I pulled into the girls' driveway and glared at the window as Nessa narrowed her eyes on the other side. She came outside as I got out of the car and stomped towards me after locking the door behind her. "I thought Natalie was picking me up."

"I was closer. Come on."

"You didn't have to do this."

"Of course, I did. I thought you said we were going to be friends," I bit out, hating myself.

She flinched but sat in the passenger seat, buckling up. "You're right. We can do this."

"You're the one who broke it off," I snarled, hating myself. This was a great way to get her back, acting like a fucking asshole.

"You're right. This is all my fault. I'm sorry." Her voice broke, and I cursed. I reached out and gripped her hand. She looked up at me, her whole body shaking. "I can't right now, Miles. We'll talk. I promise. I just can't."

"I get it," I whispered. "No, I don't actually get it, but right now isn't the time. We're going to support our friends, and we're going to make sure they know that we care about them. And then you and I will talk. We need to talk, Nessa."

She nodded, and I gave her hand one last squeeze before I pulled out onto the road, tension roaring in my gut.

"I don't know how I'm going to pay to fix my car. I don't know how I will pay to go through the last semester or do anything. We got more bills from the hospital," she said, her laugh hollow. I looked over at her as I pulled onto one of the side roads instead of getting onto the highway. My traffic app told me there was an accident on the highway, and we were going to be late if we went that way.

"Are you serious?" I asked.

She nodded. "Yep. Another hundred grand. And there will be more to come. We're already losing the house, and I honestly do not have the money to pay for the semester. I have no idea what I'm going to do. All of this... I have no idea what to do. I can't afford to fix my car; I can't afford to do anything. I should have just gone to community college and called it a day."

"Things were different when you started here," I whispered. I knew as soon as I said the words that they were the wrong thing to say.

"You're right. They were. Maybe I shouldn't have started this semester at all. I shouldn't have started a lot of things. They only hurt in the end." She looked at me, and I glanced at her out of the corner of my eye, wanting to keep my eyes on the road.

"Nessa, I..." But I didn't get to get the words out. I heard a scream, a crunching sound, and felt as if I had been thrown back in time. Back to when Rachelle had been screaming when we hit the guardrail, and everything changed.

Only it wasn't then. This was now, and it wasn't a guardrail. I hadn't let my attention wander. I was the one driving, not my twin.

No, something had hit us. Nessa screamed, and I

tried to move, tried to do anything, but there was nothing I could do.

I heard another scream, and my head smashed into the window.

And then, there was nothing.

NINETEEN

Nessa

I groaned as I fluttered my eyes open, trying to figure out what'd just happened. Everything ached, and the coppery taste of blood in my mouth told me something was wrong. Light shone in my eyes, and I closed them again, trying to catch up. Something was wrong.

A groan escaped as I lifted my lids again, trying to take in my surroundings. We were in the car. Miles and I had been talking about something I didn't remember. Miles. He had to be okay. Had we gone off the road? No, something had hit us. Right?

I turned my head, moaned, and then looked at him, my whole body shaking. Miles lay with his head against the side window, cracks in the glass, more shattered around both of us. Blood ran from a wound on his head. His eyes were closed, his body still as death at first, but then I saw his chest move. He was breathing.

"Miles," I gasped and swallowed hard.

I reached out, but I couldn't move. My seatbelt was jammed, digging into my hip. My fingers fumbled as they went to the clasp, trying to press the button. It wouldn't work. I pulled and tugged. Finally, the mechanism released, and I nearly fell forward.

I reached for Miles, afraid to move him in case he had a spinal injury, but I still had to touch his hand. To feel his warmth, his pulse.

"Miles. Wake up." Tears fell down my cheeks, and my voice was a rasp, but I needed Miles to wake up. He needed to be okay.

I looked for my phone but couldn't find it. It had been on my lap before the accident. Now, it was somewhere in the car. What the hell had happened?

Someone should have seen. Should have witnessed the accident and called 911 for us. Maybe the other driver? I looked around, and a scream wrenched from my throat.

Xander stood on the other side of the door, his face pressed against the window. He smiled.

Oh, dear God.

This was all Xander. He had run us off the road. All of this was him. Somehow, Xander had used the situation and followed us, and now we were hurt. Miles was unconscious, and Xander was here.

And I was alone.

"Call 911," I yelled, trying to plead for mercy, but I didn't think that would happen. Not with Xander. And not now.

He smiled again and opened the door. It creaked and strained against the angle the accident had bent it into.

Only the car had hit Miles' side.

Not mine.

Xander had hurt Miles. All to get to me?

What the hell was he going to do now?

"Come with me quietly, and nobody has to get hurt." He winked. "No one else, anyway. Sorry about Miles. He should've listened. I told you that you were mine. We had a great time together, Nessa love. We enjoyed one another. And then you had to go for him. It's all his fault."

"Xander," I rasped as I kicked out. "You can't do this."

He shook his head and slowly pulled something metal out of his pocket. I froze, my whole body shaking. "I don't want to have to use this," he said as he waved the gun. "We're at this corner here. Nobody's driven by in over ten minutes. They're all stuck on the highway or taking other back roads. Lucky for me that I have this moment with you. I was planning to take you out at home, but you were never alone. Then I got pinched, and well, here we are. The accident was fortuitous. Come with me. I promise, I won't shoot him. He already looks to be hurt enough, don't you think?" he asked and winked again.

I had to talk him down. There was no way I could fight back, not with the gun in his hand and the look on his face. I didn't want to die, and I sure as hell didn't want whatever Xander had planned for me. Yet, the only thing that truly mattered at the moment was Miles. I needed to lead Xander away from Miles before he changed his mind and hurt Miles even more. "Xander, you don't have to do this."

"I do. Don't you see? You didn't listen to me at the party. You didn't pay attention the way you should have. In reality, this is your fault, Nessa darling."

I didn't scream. I didn't do anything but try to catch my breath. I wasn't having an asthma attack, but it felt like one could come on at any moment. When Xander tugged at my wrist, I nearly fell out of the car, tripping over my feet. "Stop being so clumsy. You aren't going to get out of this. You were supposed to be mine. Don't you see? I am a *nice* guy. I took care of you. I was kind to you. I noticed you when no one else did. That little British friend of yours? He left you for that bitch. I was there to protect you. What did you do? You fell for the guy in glasses. I'm the one who will always be your friend and take care of you. Not this loser."

He waved the gun again before putting it in its holster at his hip. I hadn't even realized he wore one. This had to be a nightmare, but I wasn't going to wake up anytime soon.

"Now, I don't want this gun to get in the way of what I'm going to do to you," he said as he leered and tugged me towards his truck. It was a big one with a lift kit. He'd smashed it into our car and it barely looked damaged from the assault. "Get in the fucking truck, Nessa. Please don't fight or you'll regret it."

He didn't have his hand on the gun. I had time to flee if I was quick. I pulled at him, and he struck out, the back of his hand meeting my face in a blur of heat and pain.

I tripped back and fell to the ground. We were behind a pillar, bushes and trees all around. Nobody could see us from the road. Even if I screamed, I didn't think they would hear it over the sounds of the highway in the distance and the waterway behind us.

No one could hear. I needed to save myself. And Miles.

I had to get to Miles.

"I'll just get a taste here while we wait." He kicked me, and I groaned, rolling into a ball to protect my stomach. Then he looked at me and licked his lips. I screamed again and kicked at his knee. He went down. I punched his face, trying to claw at him, but I knew the best thing I could do was run.

Run and get Miles. Find my phone and call for help. There had to be something I could do. I scrambled to my feet and began running, but he pulled at my hair. I fell backward and hit the ground, my body bruising, but I didn't care. I needed to get out of there.

Again, he didn't reach for his gun. He didn't go for anything but me.

Did he forget that he had it there? I hoped he had. For all of our sakes, I hoped he forgot.

"You're going to regret you did that," he growled, and then he was on top of me, pressing his mouth to mine. I kneed him in the balls, and he shouted, falling off me. I kicked him again and again before scrambling away.

"You bitch."

"No, you're the bitch," Miles snarled from behind me. I looked up then, blood on my palms and my knees, my heart racing.

"He has a gun!"

"I don't fucking care." Miles hit Xander once. Twice. Xander just grinned as he stumbled back, but he didn't reach for that gun.

He lashed out at Miles, but Miles was quicker. They were both standing now, and Miles hit him again, and again, and again. I looked at them and then at the car. I knew my phone was in there somewhere. I needed to call for help.

"Miles, stop. Don't kill him."

"He deserves it," he growled, and I ran towards the car. My phone lay on the floorboard, and I grabbed it and called 911. Miles stood over Xander, and my stomach roiled.

"I need help. We need help," I whispered into the phone. Miles looked at me then, blinked, and then fell, his whole body sagging as whatever adrenaline he had left, disappeared in a rush. I ran towards him, towards the man who had saved me even as I tried to save him, and pushed at Xander to make sure he was out of it.

As I looked at the gun that had fallen at his side, I realized there were no bullets in it. He had threatened me with no ammunition. He didn't matter now, though. Only Miles did. I gently put Miles' head in my lap as tears streamed, and I tried to explain to the authorities where we were. I heard footsteps, other cars finally seeing us on the side of the road, the drivers coming to help. I cried and held onto Miles, hoping we could fix this.

Hoping to hell this wasn't the end.

Twenty

Miles

I leaned my head against the pillow and looked over at Pacey. My roommate had his hands steepled in front of him, resting his elbows on his knees as he stared at me.

"You scared the shit out of me," he said.

I nodded. "It scared me, too." My eyes pulsed because I had moved my head, and I told myself I shouldn't do that again. "Is she okay?" I asked, my voice soft.

I needed to know. All I could do was think about the sound of the car hitting us, the metal against metal that was so familiar. It had already echoed into my dreams for so long, and it had nothing to do with Nessa before. Now, her scream and my sister's would be forever entwined, and I wasn't sure how to deal with that.

I'd been in two car accidents in my life, both so severe that the cars had been totaled and I was afraid I would lose everything.

All I could do now was try not to throw up, thinking about what could have happened and how it could have been worse.

"Her dad took her home," Pacey said after a moment. "She got stitches on her forehead from some glass that cut her. She's bruised, but she wasn't hurt other than that. You took most of the impact."

"That asshole dragged her across the ground, Pacey. Yanked her out of that fucking car and kicked her and hurt her, and it could have been so much worse."

Pacey's jaw clenched. "It could have. It wasn't. You took care of her."

I snorted and then cursed.

"Stop doing that," Pacey said. "You're only going to hurt yourself."

"I deserve it. She saved herself, you know. She was fighting back and kicking. She didn't need me."

"That's where you're wrong," Pacey growled. "You

two saved each other. Bloody hell, I can't believe that kid did that."

"He's not a kid," I snapped, ignoring the pain. "A kid doesn't do that. We call him a kid, and we're giving him an out. An excuse. He's a grown-ass human being. A fucking man—or so he thought. He did that. He hurt her. Fuck him."

"You broke his jaw, his nose, and Nessa hurt his balls so bad, he's going to need surgery to get one pulled back or whatever. I don't want to think about what that entails."

"They should keep them inside him. That motherfucker."

"They should just castrate him for what he planned to do to her." I let out a low growl, ignoring the pain once again.

"She hurt him, but so did you. You saved each other. And that fucking wanker will never touch her or another human being again."

"I thought the cops said he was still in jail for a DUI."

"He got out on bail. Thanks to his father, I guess. That was his mother's boyfriend's truck he used to hurt you."

"So, he was following us. It's not like he orchestrated a car accident on the highway to get us to that road."

"No, it seemed to be out of the blue. Not premeditated, at least that's what other people are saying. Maybe to try to get a lesser sentence. I don't know, but I hope they throw the book at him."

"I hope they do, too. I'll do whatever I can to make that happen."

"Her dad took her home. I didn't get to talk to her," Pacey said after a moment. "I don't know what I would've said."

"You guys are still friends, you know," I said after a moment. "It was never weird between you and me, was it?"

"No. I like the two of you together. She's happy."

I nearly laughed, but I knew it would hurt, and more than just my head. "No, we weren't together. We were only pretending. Then she left me."

"Take some time. You'll figure it out."

"No, it was already too much for her before the accident. I'm not going to force myself or her into a relationship she doesn't want."

"Give yourself some time," Pacey said again. "You helped me figure out everything with Mackenzie. You help us all. You deserve her. You'll figure things out. Nessa is one of my favorite human beings. You deserve each other."

"Somehow, that doesn't sound like a curse," I said

with a soft laugh, grateful that my head didn't hurt that much this time.

"Sometimes, you guys are stubborn. But then again, so am I. I am going to go now and let everyone know you're okay. Your family's waiting, so I can't stay for long. I'm surprised they even let me in here in the first place."

I nearly sat up, but Pacey's glare stopped me. "They let me in here first, though I don't know why. They're out there, and they look scared. I'm sorry you're going through all of this."

I had told him and Dillon everything that had happened with my sister before since keeping secrets after telling Nessa and Tanner didn't work anymore. I was trying to be more open, or at least I had been before the accident.

I still couldn't believe that Nessa had been hurt. That her dad had taken her away. And I wasn't sure when I would get to see her again. I didn't know if she would stay with the girls or if she would find an apartment with her dad. Or even if she was going to stay for the semester. I didn't know anything. And all I wanted to do was hold her and tell her that everything would be okay. And then I wasn't sure that was the truth. I didn't know if I was lying anymore.

Pacey gave me a look, a tight nod, and then walked away, presumably to find the rest of my roommates. I let out a breath and looked up as my parents and Aaron walked in. My stomach clenched. The last time I'd been in the hospital, it had been because of the accident with Rachelle, and I remembered the broken looks on their faces. Their disappointment had shattered me. I didn't want to see that again. So, it took me a moment to meet their gazes. When Dad cleared his throat, I looked right at him.

There was no shame, no judgment there—just utter despair.

I didn't know what was worse.

"Mom, Dad," I whispered, and my mom let out a broken sob.

She rushed forward and gripped my hand, looking down at me as she wiped away her tears. "I'm so glad you're okay."

"I'm fine, Mom."

"We could have lost you," she said, shaking her head. "We could have lost you again. I know it wasn't your fault," she began. "The accident. Either time. And I'm so sorry. We're just so scared to lose you. We were so scared to lose you before. Now, it's even worse. I can't believe that man came after you and Nessa. I can't believe any of this."

She stood back and put her arm around Aaron's shoulders as my little brother stared at me, his eyes wide. My dad cleared his throat again and then leaned forward to brush my hair away from the stitches on my forehead. "He's locked up?" my dad asked, and I swallowed hard.

"Yes. He won't be able to hurt Nessa again."

My dad narrowed his eyes. "He won't be able to hurt you again either."

"I'm sorry," I whispered.

"It's not your fault. None of this was ever your fault," my dad whispered. "We were so afraid of losing you after we lost Rachelle that we didn't know how to control everything. We need to fix this. We need to make sure that you know we love you. We won't take Aaron away from you. I promise."

I looked up at my little brother then, my stomach hurting. "You okay?" he asked, his voice soft.

I nodded. "I'm going to be fine. Just a little banged up."

"And Nessa? She's okay?"

I swallowed hard. "She's going to be okay."

"Good."

"We're going to let you rest," my mom said, rolling her shoulders back. "Then we're going to talk. I think we have a lot of things to talk about. Things we should've discussed a long time ago. I love you, Miles."

"Same here," my dad said, his voice rough. He leaned down and kissed me, then I watched them walk away, my little brother giving me a wave—although he was nearly my mother's height, so maybe he wasn't so little anymore.

They left me alone as I lay in my hospital bed, trying to catch up. I wanted Nessa here. I wanted her to be here so I could talk this over. So I could figure out what to do about my family. Because something had just changed. I didn't know *what* exactly. Maybe we'd be able to find a way to focus on making things work.

I couldn't think about my family right now, though. Couldn't think about school or my roommates. I could only think about the girl who wasn't here. The one I feared would never take me back.

Twenty-One

Nessa

"Excuse me?" I asked as I leaned against the back of the couch. My head ached, but it wasn't from the stitches. Instead, I sat there, trying to comprehend exactly what my agent was telling me. "You have three offers, Nessa. And they're *good* offers. F*antastic* offers."

Nothing computed at the moment. "How? I wasn't expecting anything."

"I know you weren't. You never do, Nessa. You're so talented. I saw that right away, and we have a lot more things to go over, but we have time to look over everything."

"I don't understand," I whispered.

"This is *the call*, Nessa. *The. Call.* We'll make decisions and talk it over, but you're going to be okay. I promise you."

We talked some more, and as my tears threatened, I knew I would look over everything later and talk with her about every single detail, but I couldn't focus right now.

All in the span of a week, I had broken up with Miles, realized I had fallen in love with him, been attacked, hurt, and watched someone be handcuffed and taken away. I had watched Miles get put into an ambulance. I had done the same. Now, it seemed I had a fucking deal for my trilogy.

I had sold my book. I would be okay.

The next semester would still be tough, but if I knew I had some income coming in, I could use my loan and the funds from the house for the next semester and know I had money coming in the next year. It would be tight, but there was a way now.

I had a future. One I would still work hard at and continue relying on things other than just my advance. I wouldn't quit everything and pretend I was a full-time author. But I had options now.

Real options.

I could barely breathe.

My dad had gone to work since he couldn't take any more time off. He had already taken off enough with Mom, and we were only just now catching up to that.

He was working way more hours than I was, trying to keep us afloat.

The house I had grown up in was filled with boxes as my dad had found a smaller home to live in. This one would be on the market in the next week, but I had still stayed this past week, healing and just trying to be.

The girls visited, as did the guys—at least Pacey and Dillon did.

Miles hadn't come, nor had Tanner. Tanner had texted, saying that he was glad I was okay.

Technically, it had only been five days, but it felt like a full week. Miles had gotten home the day before as they had kept him for a few days because they had been worried about internal bleeding. The guys kept me up to date, but Miles had lost his phone in the accident. Mine had been taken away for evidence, and I had only recently gotten a new one, thanks to Natalie. I hadn't wanted to rely on her or anyone, but she had said that I needed a phone. I would take it, even if I didn't really like it.

I didn't know if Miles had gotten a new one yet.

I wanted to call him, tell him I was sorry. Say that I loved him and wanted to figure things out.

When I got overwhelmed, I freaked out. And I had freaked out.

I had to continue telling myself that things would be okay. My dad and I couldn't keep this house, but that was fine. The memories in it weren't the easiest to deal with anyway.

We would make do.

Only I had hurt Miles because I hadn't been able to handle it all.

The doorbell rang, and I frowned before I got up, gingerly stepping towards it because everything still hurt. I was one big bruise as if I were a dropped peach, but that's what happened when you were dragged across cement and dirt, kicked, and punched. I tried not to think about the details, though I knew I'd have to talk to someone soon. But not now. Now, I needed to see who was at the door.

My heart sped up as I looked through the peephole. I tried to blink back the tears.

I undid the two locks and opened the door to see Miles standing there. One side of his face was a bruise, and he had a busted lip, but he simply looked at me. I wanted to reach out. I wanted to fall into his arms and tell him that I was sorry, that I never wanted to let go. He had his hands in his pockets, and he looked at me, his glasses perched on the tip of his nose. "Tanner dropped me off. I can't drive yet."

"Oh." I didn't have any other words, and I felt foolish.

He let out a hollow laugh. "I don't know why I said that first. Hi, Nessa. Can I come in?"

I stepped back, and he walked through the door. I watched him move, trying to hold myself back from leaping into his arms. He had to hurt like I did, and me jumping on him probably wouldn't be the best thing for either of us.

"I wanted to see you. I wanted to give you time, but I also wanted to see you. I wasn't sure if you had your phone yet. I just got mine today, so it's been a hell of a week."

I swallowed hard. "I have my phone. Natalie got me one."

"Me, too." He laughed. "Apparently, she's just giving out phones willy-nilly."

"I think she needed something to do. When she's stressed out, she tries to take care of everyone. When I'm stressed, I run away." There. Now it was out there.

"I think I do the same thing, though I wasn't even aware I did."

I looked up at him.

"I'm so sorry," I whispered. "I'm sorry for pushing you away. For acting like I didn't need you. For thinking you were the one thing that was too much. You weren't, Miles. I'm sorry."

"Hell." He shook his head.

My stomach fell, and I nearly staggered back. "Oh," I said.

"I came over here to tell you that I love you, Nessa. That no matter what happened, I wanted to try to work things out. That I would follow whatever path brought the two of us together, no matter what else we had going on in our lives. I fucking love you so much, Nessa. It may be too soon, but I don't care. Honest to God, I don't give a fuck. You're it for me. Maybe you always have been, and it took me a while to see that. You're it. I want to see you bloom. I want to see the author and the person you become. I want to be by your side as we figure out the mess that is our lives. I want to figure it all out together. I fucking love you so much, Nessa. So, I'm here. And I'm not going anywhere."

Tears flowed freely down my cheeks, and I moved forward to cup his face, careful not to hurt his bruises. "I think I'm going to swoon, just like my heroine."

"Really?" he asked, his voice breathy.

"I love you, too. That's why I pushed you away when I did. I knew you'd always be there. And that was wrong. I got scared. I *am* scared. I'll be better if I'm with you, though. I have so much to tell you, Miles. So much that I don't know what I'm going to do about it. But no matter what, I don't want to do it without you. I pushed you away because I was afraid that once you left, it would hurt even more. So, I tried to be the one who left first. And that was wrong."

"I can go to school here. Or we can go together. We'll find a way. It's not either-or—all or nothing. There are ways to make this work."

"I know that now. I didn't want to think about it before. It was all too much. And maybe it still is, but I don't want to do this without you."

"Then don't. You don't ever have to."

He brushed his lips against mine once more, and I nearly cried, almost fell to the floor in bliss. From a single kiss. I sank into him, being gentle with him. I could barely catch up.

"I sold my book," I blurted.

He leaned back, his eyes wide. "Are you serious?

"Yes. I haven't told anyone else. I wanted to tell you first."

He smiled, the pride in his eyes staggering. "I'd say let's drink some champagne to celebrate, but I don't think either of us is allowed to drink right now."

"Once we're healed, we'll celebrate. So many things are changing, and I know the normal Nessa routine would be to keep pushing you away, to shove everyone away. But I don't want to do that anymore. I want to be with you. I want to find out how we're going to make this work. I want to make plans *with* you."

"Good, because we are going to make those plans, damn it. You and me against the world."

I kissed him again and knew he was right. Somehow, we'd make it work. It wasn't all or nothing. It wasn't this moment or all was lost.

Decisions needed to be made. Plans to take action on. And we would.

Together.

Twenty-Two

Miles

Another weekend, another house party, and yet today felt a little different. I sat in an oversized winged-back chair in the corner, sipping my club soda and lime, pretending it was something more potent. I was allowed to drink, but I was doing my best not to yet. My headache lingered, bothering me every once in a while, but I was taking it easy. People milled around, and we seemed a bit quieter than we had even a year ago.

We were all heading into the final semester of our college careers, though some younger people were here, too. Most of us were all over twenty-one and old enough to know better than to indulge too much tonight. We were enjoying ourselves, and I just wanted to get inside my bedroom with a certain somebody and *be*.

"You are scowling over here," Tanner stated as he came to my side, water in hand.

I snorted, ignoring the headache. "You're not drinking tonight? And I'm not scowling."

"You are, but I know who you're looking for. And I have to work later, so water it is."

"I swear I don't know how you work so many hours a week and still get schoolwork done."

"It's a balance. But we're making do. As always."

"Anyway, Nessa should be out soon. I think she was in the kitchen with the girls."

I frowned. "Natalie's here, too, then? I didn't know she would be here tonight. Nessa said she was busy."

Tanner shrugged, frowning. "I don't know. The other girls are in there. They count as the girls, too."

I snorted. "True."

"Anyway, I'm glad to see you up and about. Good job on passing all your classes."

"Hey, and I still kept my 4.0."

"Not everybody is as perfect and pretty as you, doll," he teased, rolling his eyes. He lifted his water in cheers before heading out of the house. I shook my head.

The girls did indeed come out of the kitchen, and Elise went straight to Dillon. My roommate wrapped his arms around her waist, looking as if he'd won the lottery. Pacey stood in another corner, speaking to his friends, all of them laughing when Mackenzie joined them. He held out his arm, and she slipped under it, fitting to his side as if she had always been there. As if Pacey had been waiting for her forever. From the way he relaxed, I knew that was likely the case. They seemed so perfect for each other. Hell, things really had changed in a year.

The scent of honey and jasmine hit my nose, and I looked up as if I'd been waiting for her all night. And, hell, I had been. Nessa came up to me and gently sat on my lap. My cock ached, but I ignored it. There would be time for that later.

"Are you taking care of yourself?" Nessa asked as she kissed my cheek.

I leaned against her and sighed. "Yes, but I'd rather be taking care of *you* upstairs."

"You're fortunate you whispered that," she said before kissing me.

Knowing that I didn't want to give everybody a show, I didn't linger, but I still enjoyed myself.

"You're feeling good?" I asked, meeting her gaze.

"I am. I'm happy that we all had that party to celebrate my book yesterday. It was nice." We'd had a roommate-only party to celebrate her book deal and would have another dinner with her dad later.

"Of course, we did. We're proud of you."

"It still doesn't feel real. None of this feels real. And your mom was so gracious about it."

I cringed. "Mom will want to read your books. I hope there's no sex in them."

"I'm not going to tell you if there's sex in them or not," she said and then laughed.

"It looks like you're finally going to let me read them, then. Just saying."

We'd had dinner with my parents and brother, Nessa bringing her father, as well. It had been awkward as hell at first until Nessa smiled and talked graphic novels with Aaron. The tension had eased immediately, and now it felt as if she and her dad had always been part of the family. Yes, my parents still needed time to change their ways, but I was ready to give them that. They were my parents and they loved me. And they were already in love with Nessa.

Both of us were waiting to hear about the University of Colorado for grad school, but we had high hopes. We'd tried for other schools, but Colorado was our top choice. I could still be in Aaron's life, and Nessa wouldn't have to leave her father.

Plus, we could be together.

We still had one more semester in undergrad and weren't moving in together until after we graduated. Dillon and Pacey were planning the same with their girls. The six of us were on the same path—or at least thinking about our futures that way.

"What do you say we go upstairs?" I asked, my voice a growl.

"I think that's a perfect idea."

I kissed her again, and somebody cheered, but I ignored them.

"Stop it," I growled as I flipped off the rest of the room.

Somebody laughed and yelled, "Get a room!"

I didn't know who said that, but I grinned. "You're right. I should."

"Miles!" Nessa squealed as I lifted her into my arms. "You're going to hurt yourself. You're supposed to take it easy."

"Oh, I'm sure I can."

Nessa blushed, burying her head against my neck as I carried her upstairs to a chorus of cheers from everyone downstairs.

"I'm going to kill you," she muttered.

"I love you, too."

"You're lucky I love you." She sighed and relaxed into my hold as we made our way to my room.

"You'd better show me why you think it's okay for us to go upstairs while everyone's still down there."

I closed my door behind us and locked it as I set her on her feet.

"I think that can be arranged." I pressed my lips to hers and knew this was the first time of many.

I hadn't expected Nessa to love me back. I hadn't expected anything.

She was my first love, my first everything. And my next, and my next, and my next.

She was my present, my future, and I sure as hell wouldn't take that for granted. Never again. So, I kissed her harder, and I breathed.

She was mine.

My next. My forever.

Consequences

Natalie

I had never been to this particular grocery store before, but it had a similar layout to most of them. I was on the other side of town, not because I needed to be here, but mostly because I didn't want to run into a friend. I was forever running into someone from school or someone who knew my parents. And a lot of people knew my parents.

I swallowed hard as I took my little handheld basket filled with bread and sandwich meat and random cupcakes that I had found that looked good and did my best not to throw up.

This was fine. This was nothing.

This was just an evening that would be a little stressful. But I would get over it.

I walked down the aisle, looking at the boxes of things I had never paid attention to before, and stood and studied the vast array of products that seemed foreign to me.

Okay, then. How did I choose? How was I supposed to do this shopping? Should I have just done this online and waited for it to show up on my doorstep in a few days, even with overnight shipping? No, probably not. I could do this. I was an adult. I had made other adult decisions. Now, here I was for this one.

I pulled out my phone and knew I couldn't do this alone. Even though I might have tried, I couldn't. I needed someone else, someone the others might not expect.

I pulled up Tanner's contact info and began a text.

Me: *We need to talk.*

And then I put my phone back into my bag, picked up a pregnancy test, set it in my basket, and headed to the register.

I took a deep breath and told myself once again that everything would be okay. Even though, knowing my luck, it most definitely wouldn't be anywhere near okay.

Next up in the ON MY OWN SERIES: My Bad Decisions

Want to read a special BONUS EPILOGUE featuring Nessa & Miles? CLICK HERE!

A Note from Carrie Ann Ryan

Thank you so much for reading **MY NEXT PLAY!**

I loved Miles and Nessa. They were messy and couldn't figure out what they wanted until the realized they could want each other. I adore them!

Next up in the ON MY OWN series?

Natalie and Tanner are in for a surprise in My Bad Decisions!

If you want to make sure you know what's coming next from me, you can sign up for my newsletter at www.CarrieAnnRyan.com; follow me on twitter at @CarrieAnnRyan, or like my Facebook page. I also have a Facebook Fan Club where we have trivia, chats, and other goodies. You guys are the reason I get to do what I do and I thank you.

Make sure you're signed up for my MAILING

LIST so you can know when the next releases are available as well as find giveaways and FREE READS.

Happy Reading!

The On My Own Series:

Book 1: My One Night

Book 2: My Rebound

Book 3: My Next Play

Book 4: My Bad Decisions

WANT TO READ A SPECIAL BONUS EPILOGUE FEATURING NESSA & MILES? CLICK HERE!

Want to keep up to date with the next Carrie Ann Ryan Release? Receive Text Alerts easily!

Text CARRIE to 210-741-8720

About the Author

Carrie Ann Ryan is the New York Times and USA Today bestselling author of contemporary, paranormal, and young adult romance. Her works include the Montgomery Ink, Redwood Pack, Fractured Connections, and Elements of Five series, which have sold over 3.0 million books worldwide. She started writing while in graduate school for her advanced degree in chemistry and hasn't stopped since. Carrie Ann has written over seventy-five novels and novellas with more in the works. When she's not losing herself in her emotional and action-packed worlds, she's reading as much as she can while wrangling her clowder of cats who have more followers than she does.

www.CarrieAnnRyan.com

Also from Carrie Ann Ryan

The Montgomery Ink: Fort Collins Series:

Book 1: Inked Persuasion

Book 2: Inked Obsession

Book 3: Inked Devotion

Book 4: Inked Craving

The On My Own Series:

Book 1: My One Night

Book 2: My Rebound

Book 3: My Next Play

Book 4: My Bad Decisions

The Ravenwood Coven Series:

Book 1: Dawn Unearthed

Book 2: Dusk Unveiled

Book 3: Evernight Unleashed

Montgomery Ink:

Book 0.5: Ink Inspired
Book 0.6: Ink Reunited
Book 1: Delicate Ink
Book 1.5: Forever Ink
Book 2: Tempting Boundaries
Book 3: Harder than Words
Book 3.5: Finally Found You
Book 4: Written in Ink
Book 4.5: Hidden Ink
Book 5: Ink Enduring
Book 6: Ink Exposed
Book 6.5: Adoring Ink
Book 6.6: Love, Honor, & Ink
Book 7: Inked Expressions
Book 7.3: Dropout
Book 7.5: Executive Ink
Book 8: Inked Memories
Book 8.5: Inked Nights
Book 8.7: Second Chance Ink

Montgomery Ink: Colorado Springs

Book 1: Fallen Ink
Book 2: Restless Ink
Book 2.5: Ashes to Ink

Book 3: Jagged Ink
Book 3.5: Ink by Numbers

The Montgomery Ink: Boulder Series:

Book 1: Wrapped in Ink
Book 2: Sated in Ink
Book 3: Embraced in Ink
Book 4: Seduced in Ink
Book 4.5: Captured in Ink

The Gallagher Brothers Series:

Book 1: Love Restored
Book 2: Passion Restored
Book 3: Hope Restored

The Whiskey and Lies Series:

Book 1: Whiskey Secrets
Book 2: Whiskey Reveals
Book 3: Whiskey Undone

The Fractured Connections Series:

Book 1: Breaking Without You
Book 2: Shouldn't Have You
Book 3: Falling With You
Book 4: Taken With You

The Less Than Series:

Book 1: Breathless With Her

Book 2: Reckless With You

Book 3: Shameless With Him

The Promise Me Series:

Book 1: Forever Only Once

Book 2: From That Moment

Book 3: Far From Destined

Book 4: From Our First

Redwood Pack Series:

Book 1: An Alpha's Path

Book 2: A Taste for a Mate

Book 3: Trinity Bound

Book 3.5: A Night Away

Book 4: Enforcer's Redemption

Book 4.5: Blurred Expectations

Book 4.7: Forgiveness

Book 5: Shattered Emotions

Book 6: Hidden Destiny

Book 6.5: A Beta's Haven

Book 7: Fighting Fate

Book 7.5: Loving the Omega

Book 7.7: The Hunted Heart

Book 8: Wicked Wolf

The Talon Pack:

Book 1: Tattered Loyalties
Book 2: An Alpha's Choice
Book 3: Mated in Mist
Book 4: Wolf Betrayed
Book 5: Fractured Silence
Book 6: Destiny Disgraced
Book 7: Eternal Mourning
Book 8: Strength Enduring
Book 9: Forever Broken

The Elements of Five Series:

Book 1: From Breath and Ruin
Book 2: From Flame and Ash
Book 3: From Spirit and Binding
Book 4: From Shadow and Silence

The Branded Pack Series:

(Written with Alexandra Ivy)

Book 1: Stolen and Forgiven
Book 2: Abandoned and Unseen
Book 3: Buried and Shadowed

Dante's Circle Series:

Book 1: Dust of My Wings
Book 2: Her Warriors' Three Wishes
Book 3: An Unlucky Moon
Book 3.5: His Choice

Book 4: Tangled Innocence
Book 5: Fierce Enchantment
Book 6: An Immortal's Song
Book 7: Prowled Darkness
Book 8: Dante's Circle Reborn

Holiday, Montana Series:

Book 1: Charmed Spirits
Book 2: Santa's Executive
Book 3: Finding Abigail
Book 4: Her Lucky Love
Book 5: Dreams of Ivory

The Happy Ever After Series:

Flame and Ink
Ink Ever After

The Tattered Royals Series:

Book 1: Royal Line
Book 2: Enemy Heir

CPSIA information can be obtained
at www.ICGtesting.com
Printed in the USA
LVHW022100081221
705641LV00014B/1869